***"Did anyone ever tell you that you look like Scarlett O'Hara?"***

Caitlin's eyes popped open.

The man's head was cocked to one side as he studied her. "The eyes are different, of course. I think Scarlett's were green in the book. Vivien Leigh's were blue in the movie, weren't they?"

Totally nonplussed, she nodded dumbly.

"Scarlett had something special about her. Just like you," he continued, for all the world as if he were talking sense.

Caitlin couldn't believe what she was hearing. No one had ever suggested there was anything special about her—certainly not about her looks. She wasn't special. She'd never been special. And for this man to say so was either a cruel joke or utter craziness.

"Caitlin, I think—" he began in his slow, deep voice.

"What you think doesn't matter," she said, edging toward the door. "You're a raving lunatic!"

Dear Reader:

*Stellar* is the word that comes to mind for this month's array of writers here at Silhouette **Special Edition**.

Launching a gripping, heart-tugging new "miniseries" is dynamic Lindsay McKenna. *A Question of Honor* (#529) is the premiere novel of *LOVE AND GLORY*, celebrating our men (and women!) in uniform and introducing the Trayherns, a military family as proud and colorful as the American flag. Each *LOVE AND GLORY* novel stands alone, but in the coming months you won't want to miss a one—together they create a family experience as passionate and moving as the American Dream.

Not to be missed, either, are the five other stirring Silhouette **Special Edition** novels on the stands this month, by five more experts on matters of the heart: Barbara Faith, Lynda Trent, Debbie Macomber, Tracy Sinclair and Celeste Hamilton.

Many of you write in asking to see more books about characters you met briefly in a Silhouette **Special Edition**, and many of you request more stories by your favorite Silhouette authors. I hope you'll agree that this month—and every month—Silhouette **Special Edition** offers you the stars!

Best wishes,

Leslie J. Kazanjian,
Senior Editor

# CELESTE HAMILTON

# Face Value

Silhouette Special Edition

Published by Silhouette Books New York

**America's Publisher of Contemporary Romance**

For my grandmother, Nina Carden,
and my mother-in-law, Mabel Powell,
because I love you both.

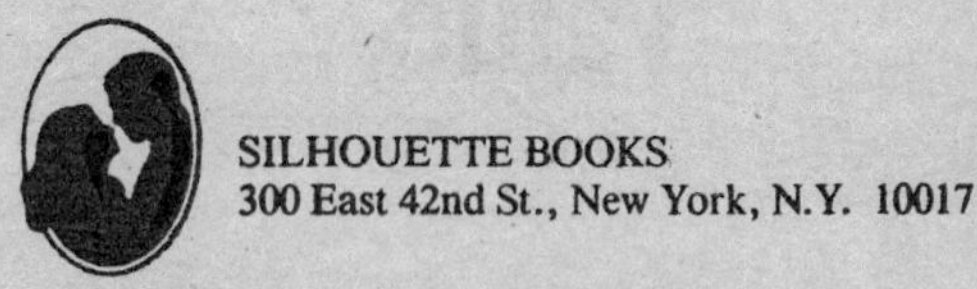

SILHOUETTE BOOKS
300 East 42nd St., New York, N.Y. 10017



ISBN: 0-373-09532-5

First Silhouette Books printing June 1989



Printed in the U.S.A.

**Books by Celeste Hamilton**

Silhouette Special Edition

*Torn Asunder* #418
*Silent Partner* #447
*A Fine Spring Rain* #503
*Face Value* #532

## *CELESTE HAMILTON*

began writing when she was ten years old, with the encouragement of parents who told her she could do anything she set out to do and teachers who helped her refine her talents. The broadcast media captured her interest in high school, and she graduated from the University of Tennessee with a B.S in communications. From there, she began writing and producing commercials at a Chattanooga, Tennessee, radio station. Aside from a brief stint at an advertising agency, she stayed with radio and now works for Chattanooga's top country music station.

Celeste began writing romances in 1985 and says she "never intends to stop." Married to a policeman, she likes nothing better than spending time at home with him and their two much-loved cats, although they also enjoy traveling when their busy schedules permit. Wherever they go, however, "It's always nice to come home to East Tennessee—one of the most beautiful corners of the world."

MISSOURI
KENTUCKY
VIRGINIA
Nashville
Knoxville
TENNESSEE
Chattanooga
NORTH CAROLINA
ARKANSAS
Mississippi River
Columbia
Atlanta
SOUTH CAROLINA
MISSISSIPPI
ALABAMA
GEORGIA
LOUISIANA
Savannah
Hilton Head Island
Atlantic Ocean
Baton Rouge
New Orleans
Gulf of Mexico
FLORIDA
SOUTHEASTERN UNITED STATES

# *Chapter One*

The night was hot and humid, typical for June in Knoxville, Tennessee, not perfect weather for scaling apartment-building walls in a suit. Nevertheless, Beau Collins eyed the wall before him with confidence and scrambled on top of a discarded crate. The wood creaked under his weight, but it held steady enough to put him level with the window he wanted.

One hard jerk freed the loose screen, and it fell to the ground. Beau grinned. As he'd expected, the window was open. He was home free. Grunting, muscles straining, he pulled himself up to the ledge and swung his legs through the opening. Then he dropped to the floor inside. At least he expected it to be the floor. It felt more like a bathtub. He turned, and his elbow sent something—shampoo bottles?—tumbling to the floor. They bounced with hollow, bathtublike echoes, but the bathtub wasn't supposed to be under the window—

*He was in the wrong apartment.*

Beau realized his mistake just as the overhead light came on. He blinked in the sudden glare and stumbled forward.

"Don't move," a woman's voice commanded.

He complied, and as his eyes adjusted to the light, a face came into focus. Not just *a* face. *The face.* Pointed chin. Determined jaw. Wide hazel eyes. The entire package framed by a cloud of unruly dark hair. After days of searching, the perfect face was staring at him—over the barrel of a gun.

*A gun,* his befuddled brain repeated. There was no need for guns. "Honest to God, lady, I'm sorry—"

"Sorry?" Her voice was shaking. So was the hand that held the snub-nosed revolver.

Just what I needed tonight, Beau thought, a nervous woman with a gun. A nervous woman with a gun and a great pair of legs, he amended, his gaze resting on the length of slender thigh revealed by her faded orange T-shirt.

"What are you looking at?" the woman snapped, reminding Beau that now wasn't the time to be admiring her legs.

"I'm sorry—"

*"You're sorry?"* Caitlin Welch squeaked in amazement. Though she had no experience with burglars, an apology was the last thing she had expected to hear. Unless this wasn't your average, garden-variety burglar. Unless this burglar was really a psychopath, some sort of weirdo who apologized just before he murdered his victims. Her imagination, fueled by what little she had seen of slasher movies, kicked into high

gear, and perspiration that had nothing to do with the heat trickled down her spine.

"This is all a stupid mistake," the man said and started to step out of the tub.

"Don't move!" Caitlin shouted again. Why in heaven's name hadn't she called the police instead of snatching the gun out of the bedside-table drawer and rushing into the bathroom? But at least she had thought to get the gun. Two years had passed since her mother had bought the weapon for her and forced her to take a firearms course. *Two years?* Caitlin hadn't touched the gun since then. She didn't even know if it was loaded. An unloaded gun would do her no good at all if this maniac turned on her. Screaming probably wouldn't help, either, since both of her upstairs neighbors were out of town. Terror gripped Caitlin again, and the room swam before her eyes.

"Are you okay?" the burglar asked, sounding oddly concerned.

"Of course I'm all right!" The hysterical note in her voice clashed with the paralyzing numbness of her brain. Where was her usual calm and logic? She ignored the thought that there was nothing calm or logical about finding a strange man in one's bathtub in the middle of the night.

The man in question was determined to talk. "I can explain if you'll—"

"Shut up and reach for the sky!" *Good heavens,* Caitlin thought, *did I really say that?*

To Beau she sounded like a woman who had seen too many reruns of *Cagney and Lacey*. This was all too strange. Laughable, really, but something told him to hold back the laughter. He didn't want the lady with the perfect face to use that gun on him. He tried once again to explain, "If you'll just listen—"

"Shut up and get your hands up." She waved the gun.

Beau raised his hands, and despite his best efforts laughter came tumbling out of his mouth. "Really," he gasped. "I can explain all this—"

"Explain it to the police."

His laughter ended and, for the first time in his life, Beau began to doubt his ability to talk his way out of a situation. "There's no need to call them," he said hastily. "I didn't mean to come in your window. I'm your neighbor—"

"My neighbor?" Her incredulous eyes opened even wider.

God, what a perfect face she has, Beau thought again. Not perfect in the classic sense, but for an advertising man in search of just the right model—as he was—her face was a salvation. To think she'd been right next door while he had been digging through modeling-agency portfolios all week. Of course none of that made any difference now, not while he was in danger of being carted off to jail. He had to make this woman understand that it was all a mistake. Then he would talk to her about her face.

He quickly gave her his name, adding, "Hunt Kirkland loaned me the apartment next door. You know he owns this building, don't you?"

"Of course," she snapped.

"Hunt and I have been friends for years," Beau continued. "We played football together in college, and he married my cousin this past February." Sensing the more details he provided, the more likely she would be to believe him, he added, "His wife, my cousin's name is Melissa. Together they run a restaurant in Chattanooga."

"And does that give you the right to break into my apartment?"

"No, but—"

"Then explain to me why you came in through my bathroom window."

The hilarity of the situation hit Beau again. "Sounds like a song, doesn't it? The wrong gender, of course—"

She blinked. "What?"

"You know, the Beatles' song, 'She Came In Through the Bathroom Window.'" He launched into the first chorus.

She cut him off by jerking the gun toward his head. "You're crazy, aren't you?"

The gun was beginning to make Beau nervous again. "I told you," he said earnestly, "I'm your neighbor."

"And that means you can't be crazy?"

He hesitated. "Strictly speaking, no, but—"

The frightened look crept back into her eyes. "I think we're going to go in the other room and call the police now, okay? I'm sure they'll take you back where you belong."

"But I belong next door," Beau insisted. "I've been going in and out for the past week. You have to have seen me."

Caitlin squinted at the intruder, and he came into sharper focus. Without her glasses it was hard to be sure, but there was something vaguely familiar about him. Was it yesterday or the day before that she had stood at the window and watched a red-haired man get into his car outside the apartments? She had assumed it was her new neighbor, but she hadn't given him much thought or attention. With everything that had been on her mind this lonely, frustrating week, she hadn't felt like thinking about neighbors. In fact she'd been lost in her problems—tossing and turning and trying to sleep—when she'd heard the crash from the bathroom.

"You recognize me, don't you?" Beau asked, pleased to see the gun lowering.

Caitlin snapped it back up. "That doesn't explain what you're doing in my bathtub."

"I thought it was mine."

"What?"

He looked sheepish. "I got home tonight and realized my door key was in my apartment. I was pretty sure I could get in through my bathroom window, so I went around back and mistakenly thought your window was mine. It's dark outside."

"It's usually dark at midnight," Caitlin observed dryly.

"Is it that late? Damn, I'm sorry. I hope I didn't wake you."

She couldn't stop her sarcastic retort. "No, I normally stay awake all night. One never knows who's going to drop into the bathtub."

He laughed again. The sound rolled out of him as easily as his Southern drawl. It was a pleasant laugh, not at all the sort she'd expect from a murderer or rapist. Maybe he was telling her the truth.

"Can I put my arms down now?" he asked.

"I guess so."

He let his arms drop and flexed his hands. "And can I get out of the tub?" She nodded and he stepped out, eyeing her warily. "Are you going to keep pointing the gun at me?"

Caitlin wavered but kept the gun aimed at him. No matter how pleasant he sounded, he might still be dangerous. There had to be something wrong with a person who could act so calm and collected under these circumstances.

"Okay," he said. "I guess I don't blame you for being nervous."

"Big of you to understand."

Beau grinned. At least she had a sense of humor. "You're not still planning to call the police, are you?"

She hesitated. "I don't know."

"I know you have every right not to trust me, but I really thought your window was mine. Anyone could have made the mistake."

The faint lifting of her eyebrows was skeptical.

"All right, all right," Beau admitted. "Maybe not everyone would be trying to crawl in their window at this time of night."

"No kidding—"

"But I'm not some kind of weirdo or thief or anything else. You could make sure of that by calling Hunt."

"At midnight?"

"It's Friday night. I'm sure he's still at the restaurant."

She paused for just a moment before agreeing. "Maybe you're right. Let's go to the living room." She gestured with her gun. "Down the hall to the right."

Feeling like a wrongly accused suspect being led before a firing squad, Beau preceded her down the hall. She snapped on lights as they went. Her apartment was long and narrow and nothing like his, but individuality was one of the advantages of living in a remodeled house. And, he thought wryly, the disadvantage was that if you weren't familiar with the building's layout you could get confused about the location of a bathroom window.

But the window mix-up could turn out to be the luckiest mistake he had made in a long time. In the living room Beau assessed his neighbor again. She picked up a pair of glasses from the coffee table and put them on. The owlish frames were at odds with her long, sexy tangle of hair, and Beau thought she had the incongruous look of a school librarian caught in her underwear. Or maybe no underwear at all. He studied her slender figure even more intently. He'd lay odds she wore very little under that loose T-shirt of hers.

Now that Caitlin was no longer hampered by nearsightedness, she could see every expression that crossed her captive's face. And she didn't miss his frankly male appraisal. Wishing she had thought to put on her robe, she flushed. Men seldom looked at her this way. Especially not men who were this handsome.

Why didn't I pay attention when I saw him before? she asked herself. Her failure to do so proved just how preoccupied she'd been. Any woman in a normal state of mind would have taken in every detail of his appearance. He had red hair. And he was a hunk—tall and tan, with strong, even features and only a sprinkling of a redhead's requisite freckles. He had the sort of broad shoulders one doesn't acquire by sitting in an office, although his tailored gray suit would look just fine behind a big mahogany desk. He had the look of confidence that could carry a person through any situation, including one as crazy as this. Friend of the landlord's or not, he wasn't the sort of man she would expect to live in her modest apartment building—or to come through her window.

"I take it you've decided to trust me," he said.

"What?"

He pointed to the gun she had lowered again.

Caitlin gave it a rueful glance. "I suppose no one would make up a story like yours. And you're not dressed for breaking into a building like this. We don't have much rare art or jewelry around here."

"Is there a dress code for burglars?"

"Well, Cary Grant in *To Catch a Thief*..." Caitlin paused, realizing the absurdity of what she was saying. "How do you do that?"

"Do what?"

"Keep shifting the conversation to songs and dress codes and such nonsense."

His smile reached all the way to his green eyes, eyes fringed by surprisingly long, dark lashes that matched his eyebrows. Quite a contrast to his bright hair. "I've been told that taking over conversations is my greatest talent," he murmured, holding her gaze.

Caitlin's fingers tightened on the cool metal of her gun. "I suppose you can talk your way out of anything," she murmured. He had certainly talked her out of calling the police.

He didn't even blink. "I can assure you I've never had to talk my way out of a neighbor's bathtub before."

She tried to relax, but he made her too nervous. If only he would stop looking at her in that disturbing, intense way. She attempted to brush away her feeling of unease by summoning up a smile. "This has to be the most ridiculous situation I've ever been in. Either that or I'm dreaming."

"A Hitchcockian nightmare?"

A fresh tingle of fear moved through Caitlin. In a Hitchcock movie the most terrifying events happened when one least expected them, when the hero or heroine thought they were safe at last. Was this man waiting to spring something on her?

As though sensing her hesitation, he said, "Why don't you call Hunt?" He turned toward the end table where the phone sat. "Or I can call him for you."

"No," Caitlin said, snatching her address book from the table. "I've got the number right here."

"Suit yourself." He sat down, making himself and his expensive suit at home on her seen-better-days sofa.

Hunt Kirkland was still at his Chattanooga restaurant, and he was happy to put Caitlin's fears to rest. He had loaned the apartment to Beau, who was indeed a tall redhead, a cousin to Hunt's wife, a man who wasn't moonlighting as a cat burglar—at least as far as Hunt knew. He assured Caitlin that climbing through the wrong window at midnight was quite normal behavior for Beau.

"Beau's not what you would call predictable. He'll probably be an interesting neighbor," Hunt told her, laughing. "Let me talk to him. I can't have him scaring off my only long-term tenant."

While Beau talked with Hunt and ran up her long-distance phone bill, Caitlin went to her bedroom, put her gun away and pulled on some sweatpants. They were still talking when she returned to the living room.

Impatiently, she paced to the door, considering the improbability of a friendship between Hunt Kirkland

and this Beau Collins. Not that Hunt was staid. He was young and successful, and she had always liked him. She knew this four-unit apartment building near the University of Tennessee campus was just an investment to him, but he had been good about repairs and renovations. They had become friendly over the years, and he had made several contributions to the school where she taught. But if Beau Collins was a sample of Hunt's friends, then maybe he wasn't the sensible, sane man she had always imagined him to be.

She had her door open by the time Collins got off the phone. "It's been nice meeting you. Good night."

He rose from his seat on her couch and ambled toward her. "I get the feeling you want me to leave."

"No joke."

"I really am sorry about this." His perfect smile was full of apology. And charm. Way too much charm. Unused to such attention from men, Caitlin stood uncertainly in the doorway, wishing he would just leave. "It was never my intention to upset anyone," he added as he leaned one shoulder against the wall beside the door.

"You're lucky I didn't blow your head off," she said.

"I don't think you could."

She bristled. He had a lot of nerve. "You don't know what I could do."

"Oh, come now. You had several opportunities to shoot me, and you didn't."

"I wish I had called the police."

"If you want my advice—"

"I don't—"

He ignored her interruption. "The next time a strange man lands in your bathtub, you *should* call the police."

"I'm hoping I won't have this problem again."

"Then you should close your windows at night. It was easy to get in here. And I'm an amateur."

Caitlin breathed an exasperated sigh and pushed at the hair that clung to her perspiring forehead. The heat was oppressive in the tiny vestibule that separated her apartment from his. It was too hot to stand around arguing. "I happen to like fresh air, Mr. Collins."

"Please call me Beau."

"All right, Beau," Caitlin replied, emphasizing his name. "I like leaving my windows open, and I like a good night's sleep—something I'm not getting this evening." Once more she gestured toward the hallway.

But Beau didn't move. The more he saw of her, the more certain he was that she was perfect for the Plantation House Resort ad campaign. But how could he bring up the subject? They had not gotten off to the best of starts, and that was not his usual way with women. He'd have to do something about it. Right now. "I really am sorry," he repeated, summoning what he hoped was his most winning smile. "But we still have a problem."

"What's that?"

"I'm still locked out of my apartment."

"I'm sure you can call the rental agency tomorrow and get a key."

"What do I do tonight?"

"That's your problem, not mine."

He smiled even wider. "Now is that a neighborly attitude?"

Still standing at the open door, Caitlin shifted from foot to foot while her irritation faded. With that smile he could alter a mood as easily as he changed the course of a conversation. Her anger was disintegrating, leaving her with a potent awareness of the man who lounged so casually against her wall. He looked so...so...*male*. An utterly masculine note in a room that hadn't known a man's presence for a long time. And he was studying her with that intense, knowing gaze again. Knowing? she repeated to herself. What could he know about a woman like her?

He stepped closer, his smile broadening. "How about it? Could you lend me a flashlight and help me find the right window?"

Caitlin would never have expected herself to do as he asked. Sensible women didn't follow handsome strangers into dark alleys in order to hold a flashlight and assist in the destruction of a window screen. But she had never tangled with a smile as persuasive as Beau Collins's. And there was nothing about this night that fit the sensible pattern of her life. So she soon found herself in the alley, the beam of her flashlight following him as he disappeared through his own bathroom window.

On the way back inside, she paused to look up at the dark expanse of moonless sky and to take a deep, steadying breath. "What would Mother think if she could see this?" she wondered out loud. Then she smiled. Beverly Welch, who often begged her daughter to be a little more impulsive, would be beaming and suggesting ways for Caitlin to prolong this encounter with the handsome redhead.

But even her mother wouldn't have predicted that Beau Collins would be waiting in the hall by their front doors, still wearing that intoxicating smile. "I can't begin to thank you for your help tonight."

"You're wel...come," she said, tripping over the word. Less than an hour ago she had been pointing a gun at this man. Now they were exchanging pleasantries in the hall. With a tiny shake of her head, she opened her door.

"Would you like to come over and have a beer or something?"

His invitation took her by surprise. She stared up at him, more tempted than she cared to admit. "Mr. Collins—"

"Beau," he insisted.

She took a deep breath and started again. "It's late, and—"

"Don't tell me you'll be able to sleep after all this excitement. You're not really sleepy are you, Caitlin?"

His exaggerated, teasing drawl gave her name an entirely new flavor, one that caused a disturbing reaction in the pit of her stomach. "I don't remember telling you my name," she said, disliking the nervous catch in her voice.

"You said it when you called Hunt, remember?"

She didn't remember, but she nodded anyway.

"Hunt said you're a teacher, and—"

"You asked him about me?" Immediately, she yearned to recall the eager, breathless words.

"Yes, and since you're a teacher and tomorrow's Saturday, you can stay up a little later tonight."

"Actually, I'm not working at all this summer," Caitlin confessed, wondering why she thought he would care.

"Then you've got not excuses, Caitlin." Again her name poured from his lips like sweet, slow molasses. "What do you say to a beer? You know you can't go back to sleep right now."

He was right. If she went to bed she'd probably just resume her tossing and turning and worrying. But she didn't frequent men's apartments, and she didn't like beer, so she really had no logical excuse for accepting his invitation. If she couldn't sleep she could always watch television or read, although both of those activities were less than appealing when compared with this man's smile. She could almost feel her mother nudging her forward as she gave in to the impulse and said yes.

"Come on," he said and opened his door. "I've got something I want to talk to you about."

Caitlin couldn't imagine what he could possibly want to discuss with her, but moments later she was seated on his couch taking a sip from a glass of beer he'd poured her. She grimaced at the bitterness, put the glass on the table and waited for Beau to say whatever it was he had to say.

But all he could do was slouch into a canvas-backed director's chair and stare at her with the same strange expression he had been displaying all evening.

Caitlin bore his perusal for only a minute or two. "I wish you would stop looking at me like that and tell me—"

"Take off your glasses."

"What?"

"Your glasses." He was out of his chair and had pulled her to her feet before she could protest.

He pulled the frames from her face, tossed them on the coffee table and leaned close enough for her to see the faint shadow of his beard. Close enough for her to catch his musky-male scent. Her heart slammed against her rib cage, knowing this was it—the surprise twist that came in every Hitchcock film. Closing her eyes, she waited for him to do to her all the unspeakable things that madmen do to innocent trusting women in the movies.

An eternity of waiting passed before he spoke. "Did anyone ever tell you that you look like Scarlett O'Hara?"

Caitlin's eyes popped open. Her breath came out in a loud gasp, but she couldn't formulate any reply.

His head was cocked to one side as he studied her. "The eyes are different, of course. I think Scarlett's were green in the book. Vivien Leigh's were blue in the movie, weren't they?"

She nodded, although she had no idea what he was talking about.

"And in the book Scarlett wasn't really conventionally beautiful, was she?"

She gaped at him. What was he getting at?

He answered his own question, still regarding her thoughtfully. "Scarlett just had something special about her. Just like you."

It was difficult for Caitlin to believe what she was hearing. No one had ever suggested there was anything special about her—at least not about her looks. True, she had reasonably good skin and an okay smile. But her eyes were too big for her face. Her hair was long and thick and so untamable that she usually just twisted it up in a bun. And her body was more angled than curved, not voluptuous enough to rate a second look from most men. She wasn't special. She'd never been special. And for this man to say so was either a cruel joke or just utter craziness.

"Caitlin, I think—" he began in his slow, deep voice.

"What you think doesn't matter," she muttered, edging backward toward the door. "Because you are a raving lunatic."

Later, Caitlin was never sure how she got to her apartment. All she remembered was slamming her door in Mr. Beau Collins's face. Though he had followed her, trying to explain, she turned the dead bolt, shut and locked all her windows and sat down on the couch, trembling.

She should never have gone to the man's apartment. Despite what Hunt Kirkland had said, Beau Collins obviously had a problem. He wasn't normal. Normal people didn't crash through neighbors' windows or compare women they barely knew to famous fictional characters. Caitlin should have used her head and turned his invitation down flat. Was she so desperate for a man's company that she was drinking beer at midnight with a stranger who had broken into her apartment? No thanks. Never again. So much for doing what her mother might have advised and being impulsive.

She wasn't going to live next door to that madman, either. Tomorrow, she'd just have to call Hunt Kirkland and tell him it was either his friend or her—one of them had to go. Still fuming, Caitlin started for her bedroom, pausing by the mirrored panel beside her front door.

She rarely looked in any mirror other than the one over the bathroom sink. This mirror had come with the apartment and successfully made the small room appear larger. For that reason Caitlin had left it up. But she usually ignored it. Now she stared into it.

The heat and humidity had made her hair even wilder than normal, and her oversize T-shirt and sweatpants hung on her body. She looked thin and pale and tired and not in the least like the legendary mistress of Tara. The man next door was nuts, or drunk or hallucinating—or all three.

However, she couldn't stop staring at her reflection, and she allowed herself what was—for Caitlin—an entirely frivolous thought. What if he did see something special in her?

Telling herself not to be silly, she spun away from the mirror, snapped off the room's overhead light and started toward the lamps. Only one man had ever seen anything attractive in her. And Tom had been gone for a year.

Only a year. It seemed more like a decade since Tom Leland had waltzed in and out of her life. The wound had healed, although her mother accused Caitlin of still pining for him. She did think of him—but without pain. In the year since he had left her, there'd been plenty of sharper, fresher pain to replace any he might have caused.

Restless pacing brought Caitlin back to the sofa, and she sat thinking about the past year. What a year. Tom had left. Julie had died. And Caitlin had buried herself in the problems of her students. She had buried herself too deep, lost her objectivity. As a consequence, she had people concerned. Her mother. The fellow teachers who were her friends. The parents of the Down's syndrome children she worked with. She had a special feeling for those children, and she couldn't let them down. That's why, instead of working in summer camp as she usually did, she had just suffered through the first week of a mandatory vacation.

Her supervisor had ordered the vacation, and Caitlin knew it was for the best. But she didn't know how to relax. She had always been so busy—helping her mother care for Julie, working her way through school, teaching at the Curtis Foundation. What was she supposed to do for two months? And after that, how was she going to go back and face all their problems again?

Those questions were echoing in her head when a knock sounded at her door. *Beau Collins.* Caitlin shut her eyes, willing him to go away. He didn't.

"Caitlin," he called through the door. "You left your glasses over here."

She sighed, surprised to realize her irritation with the man next door was gone. He was a little unconventional, maybe, but he was the landlord's friend. It wouldn't be him that had to move, so it was best for Caitlin to try to get along with him. Wearily she trudged over and opened the door.

"Hi," he said in a too-cheerful voice. "You left your glasses and your beer."

"Thanks, but you can keep the beer. Good night." Caitlin took her glasses and started to close the door.

He stopped her. "I'd like to explain about what I said before."

"Mr. Collins—"

"Please."

She sighed. What was it about this man that she couldn't resist? "Okay," she said, stepping back so he could come inside.

Relieved, Beau watched her take a seat opposite the couch. Now he was going to have to do some fancy footwork. Because he needed Caitlin's face. He had only four days in which to come up with a model for the Plantation House Resort chain's proposed campaign. Four days to find a face that would meet the exacting requirements of the chain's admittedly eccentric but oh-so-wealthy founder and owner, one Mr. Dalton Richter. Four days to save his advertising agency from extinction.

Beau took a seat on her threadbare sofa and smiled across at Caitlin. The room was dimly lit, so it was hard to read her expression. But he suspected she wasn't in the mood for chitchat. He got right down to business. "You really do look like Scarlett O'Hara."

Her laugh was derisive. "I don't look like anyone except my Great-Aunt Mabel."

"That's not true."

"Just tell me what the point of all this is."

He took a deep breath. "I've got this client, and he's got this thing about *Gone With The Wind.*"

"A client?" She sat up straighter, her voice sharpening. "What kind of client?"

"A very important one."

She made an odd, strangled sound. "The kind who wants someone to meet him in a seedy motel and dress up in hoop skirts?"

Confused, he stared at her for a moment before her words sunk in. *She thought he was a pimp!* Beau had been accused of many things but never that, and he couldn't stop his laughter.

"What's so funny?" Caitlin demanded.

"You..." Beau choked out. "You don't have much faith in me, do you?"

"Your actions since I met you tonight haven't been exactly inspiring."

"Give me a break, will you? This client owns a group of hotels and resorts—"

Caitlin jumped up from her chair. "I don't care how rich he is. I'm not interested in your dirty little business."

"But I'm in the advertising business," Beau protested, his laughter dying as he charged to his feet. "And this is a major client."

"For whom you're trying to fulfill some sort of weird fantasy, right?"

"No, no, no!" Frustrated, Beau ran a hand through his hair. "I own an advertising agency, and I'm looking for a model for a series of ads." He dug through his pocket and handed her one of his cards.

She studied it for a moment, and looked a little less sure of herself. "Okay, so you're not a pimp. But I'm not a model, either, so we can just forget—"

"You could be a model for these ads."

"For the *Gone With the Wind* freak?"

"Right."

"I guess he's going to be in the ads, too, wearing a white suit, a Panama hat and smoking a cheroot?"

Beau hid his smile. Her description of the flamboyant Mr. Richter was remarkably on target. "Not exactly. But I need a Scarlett for his ads. You could do it."

Throwing her hands up in the air, she marched back to the door. "For the third time, Mr. Collins, good night."

"Caitlin, you could do it. I promise you could."

She wheeled around to face him again and tossed her head. "This is ridiculous."

"Let me prove it to you."

"How?"

"You could do a session with a photographer I know."

"Next you'll be telling me that you can make me a star."

Beau laughed. She wasn't convinced, but at least she wasn't screaming at him anymore. "I wouldn't insult your intelligence with a line like that."

"You're insulting me with all this nonsense. I don't look like a model.

"I don't want you to look like a model. I want you to look like you."

Caitlin started to laugh, but the expression on his face stopped her. He was serious. Maybe his eyesight was impaired. Or he was being incredibly cruel. "I think you're teasing me," she said after they had stared at each other for several long moments.

"I wouldn't do that."

For reasons Caitlin couldn't quite fathom, she believed him. Why in God's name did she trust this man?

"Here," he said, taking hold of her arm.

"What are you doing?"

"I want you to look in this mirror." Gently, he turned her so that she looked into the mirror beside her door.

This mirror's getting a lot of use tonight, Caitlin thought, reluctantly doing as he said. With the harsh overhead light off she did look better than she had before. The lamp beside the sofa spread subdued shadows throughout the room. Maybe it was those shadows that softened the planes of her face. Or maybe it was the man who stood beside her, his hand on her shoulder, his gaze meeting hers in the mirror.

He bent closer, close enough for her to feel the hard muscles of his chest against her arm. With his other hand he lifted her chin so that the dim light spilled across her cheekbones. An emotion Caitlin didn't want to identify rippled through her. She watched her eyes widen and felt the warmth rush to her cheeks.

"See that?" Beau Collins whispered as his hand fell away from her chin. "Now that's quite a face."

Perhaps the light tricked her, or maybe she just wanted to see herself as he was imagining her, but for a moment Caitlin agreed with the disturbing stranger at her side. It *was* quite a face.

"I want my photographer to take your picture tomorrow."

She blinked, and the world fell back into place. The face in the mirror was nothing special at all. "I don't think so."

"Please."

She shook her head.

"Why not?"

"I've never done anything like this."

Beau decided to challenge her. A woman who could confront a burglar with gun in hand had too much spirit to resist a direct challenge. "Do you only plan to do the things you've always done?"

Her head snapped up, and her eyes were bright as they met his.

"Why not do something out of the ordinary?"

His words were a faint echo of what Caitlin's boss had said when he had given her the summer off. "Go out and kick up your heels a little," Dr. Donelson had urged her. "Have an adventure or two."

She wavered, and Beau's eyes softened. "Please," he repeated. "If you don't photograph well, all you'll have done is wasted some time."

Throughout most of her twenty-six years, Caitlin had possessed little time to waste on herself. But she did now. What was she going to do with these two months off if she didn't take a few risks?

She turned away from the mirror and faced him. "Okay. I'll have my picture taken, but that's as far as it will go. I'm no model."

"We'll see about that."

"You'll see that I'm right."

"I doubt it." Without thinking, Beau slid his hand through her hair. His fingers caught in the tangled curls, and he drew in a sharp breath. Regarding him with those huge, catlike eyes of hers, she didn't move.

In that moment he realized how hot it was in her apartment. Hot and still and filled with the sweet smell of flowers. Her scent. It drew him forward, and for half a heartbeat Beau thought about lowering his mouth to hers. But he hesitated, and that was his undoing.

Her lips looked willing enough, parted as they were and poised just a gesture away from his own. Maybe they were too willing. Maybe the yearning he could read in her eyes made her too vulnerable. Beau suspected Caitlin Welch knew very little about the needs that could draw strangers together in the darkness. Her face held just that sort of innocence. Briefly he considered turning that innocence to his advantage. If he kissed the want out of her eyes, she might be more agreeable about posing for the Plantation House ads. He was immediately ashamed of himself. He wasn't that sort of user. His hand left Caitlin's hair, and he stepped backward. "It's late," he murmured and turned away.

Caitlin stood still, wondering if the last few moments were the beginning of the adventure Dr. Donelson had urged her to have this summer.

Beau was scribbling something on the notepad Caitlin kept beside her telephone. "The address of my photographer," he explained, handing the paper to her. "Do you know where this is?"

She nodded.

"Can I call you in the morning with the time?"

"Sure."

"Great." Beau's eyes slid away from hers as he opened the door. "I'll see you there." There was no trace of his compelling smile as he went into his own apartment.

Caitlin's good-night stuck in her throat as the door across the hall closed with a firm click. She stared at it for a moment and then shut her own. Before she turned out the lights, she lingered in front of the mirror, trying to catch a glimpse of what Beau Collins said he saw in her.

In his own bathroom Beau splashed some water on his face, and for the second time that evening, he stared at his reflection in a mirror. He felt as if it were his father staring back at him. The feeling was more than mere resemblance. He felt like his father. Faced with the same business problems Beau had, his father would have used any means at his disposal to get Caitlin to do what he wanted. His father would have kissed her, used her. The fact that Beau had considered doing the very same thing gave him the uncomfortable suspicion that he was his father's son, after all. And that was one ambition Beau had never possessed.

When had his business become the center of his world? That was exactly the kind of attitude he had promised himself he would never have. His father would sacrifice everything for the family firm. Beau had never wanted to live his life that way. He *wasn't* going to live that way.

For that reason he wouldn't use the woman next door. He'd lose the Plantation House account and lose his agency first. He'd risk failure and face the I-told-you-so looks in his parents' eyes before he ever stooped so low.

Risk failure? The failure of his business was more certainty than risk if he didn't win the Plantation House account. And four years of work would go down the drain.

It didn't seem possible that this time last year he had been sitting on top of the world. From a home base in Chattanooga, his agency had been directing accounts all over the Southeast. He had even opened a second office here in Knoxville. Then his two major clients jumped ship, lured away by a big agency in Atlanta. Another client had gone bankrupt.

For the briefest of moments, Beau had thought he might have been better off if he had joined the prestigious family law firm and pursued the career in politics his parents had dreamed of for him. But that defeatism had been fleeting. He had fought back. True, he had cut his staff, but they had won several smaller accounts in Chattanooga and Knoxville. Now all he needed was that one big account. Beau was focusing all his energy on the Plantation House Resort chain, headquartered in Knoxville. He knew he could win this client.

All he needed was the right face.

The face of the woman who was living next door.

Once again Beau thought of that moment when he had almost kissed Caitlin Welch. God, it was low of him to even think of using sexual attraction to get her help. He wasn't that desperate. Or was he? Disgusted, he turned away from his reflection in the mirror and made his way to bed.

Maybe her face wasn't the one he needed. Maybe her photographs wouldn't turn out the way he expected, and he wouldn't be tempted to use her for business purposes. And maybe when he got to know her he wouldn't be tempted at all.

Beau remembered that thought the next morning as he stood in Pete Foley's photography studio and looked at Caitlin. At least he thought it was Caitlin. It was hard to be sure since the luxuriant hair of last night was scooped back in the severest of buns. No excitement colored her cheeks or brightened her hazel eyes. The soft T-shirt had given way to a prim and proper high-necked blouse and a very long, very drab navy blue skirt. The transformation was amazing. This woman wasn't tempting at all.

"My God, Caitlin," he murmured, aghast. "What have you done to yourself?"

She came to life then, eyes snapping, cheeks flaming, revealing the same sort of spirit that had captivated him last night. And Beau knew if she'd had her gun, this time she really might have shot him.

## *Chapter Two*

*So now he realizes his mistake.* With that thought, anger spread through Caitlin. But not anger at Beau. She was angry with herself, furious that she had allowed his unexpected flattery the night before to turn her head.

Granted, last night had been unusual. It isn't every evening that a charming, handsome stranger drops through a girl's bathroom window and tells her she could be a model. But that was no excuse for Caitlin to lose her grip on reality. Just because Mr. Beau Collins had been suffering from delusions last night didn't mean she had to join him in fantasyland.

She'd suspected it was all a mistake this morning when she had again faced the same old Caitlin in the mirror. She was questioning her sanity by the time Beau called and told her what time to meet him at the photographer's studio. And now, with Beau and two other strangers staring at her in bug-eyed wonder, she realized the magnitude of her mistake.

"I told you I wasn't a model," she said, lifting her head to what she hoped was a proud angle.

Beau's expression quickly changed from horrified to speculative. It was the same way he had looked at her last night, and it made Caitlin feel like an insect on display in a science project. Only the thumbtacks pinning her to a Styrofoam block were missing.

"I'll just be going—" She turned to leave, but Beau caught her arm and brought her around to face him.

"You can't go."

"Yes I can." Caitlin pulled her arm away. She had already learned to expect the unexpected when he got that peculiar gleam in his eye, and she'd had enough excitement for one twenty-four-hour period. "I think you will agree that we've both made a mistake."

"No we haven't." Once again he took hold of her arm and propelled her toward the other two people in the loftlike room. "Caitlin Welch, this is the best photographer I know, Pete Foley, and his assistant and wife, Brenda." Caitlin could only sputter a greeting before he thrust her at Brenda. "Just some light makeup, okay?"

Brenda was as short and blond as her husband was tall and dark. She smiled at Caitlin, but her glance at Beau was uncertain. "What about wardrobe?"

"Leave her in what's she got on. It's—"

"Now wait a minute," Caitlin objected.

"What?"

"I...uh...I..." For the life of her, Caitlin couldn't focus on what she was objecting to, except maybe being talked about as if she weren't in the room.

"Beau, are you sure about this?" Pete was studying Caitlin, his doubt as clear as his full, black beard. She forced herself not to squirm under his regard.

"I know you're the master photographer, but just trust me on this one, okay?" Beau turned back to Brenda. "Let's get to the makeup. I'd like some test shots to show Richter this afternoon."

"What?" Pete stared at Beau in horror. "You know I can't have them ready. I told you—"

Beau grinned and patted him on the back. "Come on, Pete. I know you can do it."

"Can't you get them Monday? Doesn't the guy take the weekend off?"

"Are you kidding?"

"I can't do it, Beau."

"Pete, you've always come through for me. Think of what this nice fat assignment is going to mean to your business this summer. Think of—"

"All right, all right." Muttering to himself, Pete strode across the room and started adjusting lights.

Beau was talking about backgrounds and angles and filters while Caitlin was led behind a curtained partition. She took a seat in front of a lighted vanity, grumbling, "It's good to know I'm not the only person Beau can manipulate with a smile."

Brenda's laugh was easygoing. "He's just a take-charge kind of guy."

"More like a steamroller."

"In his business he can't afford to be any other way."

"Is he good at his business?"

Blue eyes twinkling, Brenda draped a sheet around Caitlin's shoulders. "Honey, Beau Collins is good at anything he sets his mind to do."

There was no opportunity to question that rather intriguing reply. Brenda was too busy with creams, powders and brushes. Light makeup obviously meant something more to her than the touch of lipstick and blush Caitlin had expected. But the result was...well, Caitlin wasn't sure. Her glasses had been tossed aside, and her image in the mirror was fuzzy. For the first time she regretted not wearing the contacts her mother had insisted she buy a few months ago.

After one last stroke of mascara, Brenda called out, "What about her hair, Beau?"

"Leave it to me."

His terse reply sent Caitlin's hands groping nervously to her rather untidy bun. What was he going to do with her hair? Heart pounding, she followed Brenda out from behind the curtain. Except for the lights around the backdrop, the room had been dimmed, and Caitlin had to blink. She focused on the glowing sign that read Darkroom on a door opposite where she stood.

"Over here," Beau called from the other direction. He soon had her seated on a bench in front of the camera.

Without ceremony he lifted her chin and studied her face. It was impossible to tell whether or not he liked what he saw. He seemed different today. The suit had been replaced by jeans and a white polo shirt, but the clothes didn't make the difference. It was his manner. The smile and the obvious charm were missing. He was crisp. All business. Caitlin swallowed. The unconventional but charming stranger of last night had made her less nervous than this no-nonsense person.

"You don't have to look so terrified," he murmured. He grinned, his green eyes crinkling at the corners, and she was reassured. His smile was the same as last night.

Her answering grin was just beginning when he started to pull the pins from her hair. She cried out in surprise. "What are you doing?"

"Unwrapping the package," he whispered. Then his hands were in her hair, scattering the pins, spreading the cloud of unruly curls onto her shoulders.

"But my hair—"

"—is beautiful," Beau finished for her. Why would anyone want to hide hair like this? Black as sin. As alive as silk in a breeze. Hair like this should be touched. Tempted, he once again spread his fingers through the ends. Yes, her hair felt just as it had last night, just as he had remembered, and the contact once more sparked a response within him. He turned away before the feeling became anything he could identify.

"Shake your head," he ordered Caitlin.

"What?"

He faced her again. "Shake your head."

Her mouth set in a stubborn line, and she gave a tiny shake of her head.

"Come on, Caitlin," he wheedled. "Get in the spirit of things. Shake out your hair."

"Why?"

"Because I said so."

Caitlin felt twin spots of furious color burn into her cheeks. "Did someone die and make you king?"

The teasing light was gone from his eyes. "No, but a little cooperation would be appreciated."

*"A little cooperation?"* she sputtered. *What had she been doing if it wasn't cooperation? This was all a favor to him!*

"Come on, we don't have all day," he taunted, moving behind Pete at the camera.

And Caitlin shook her hair, shook it until the room was spinning. When she stopped she glared at Beau, and the camera's shutter clicked, not once but several times.

Pete chuckled. "Beau, my friend, I'm beginning to see what you were talking about with this lady." He snapped two more pictures in quick succession.

"But I'm not ready," Caitlin protested.

"Sure you are," Beau said shortly. "Turn your head to the left. And to the right." Like a rapid-fire gun, the shutter began to click again.

"I think we need some mood music," Brenda called from somewhere in the surrounding darkness.

Sexy, pulsating jazz spilled out of the speakers, and for Caitlin the experience took on all the characteristics of a dream. There was Beau barking instructions at her. Raise her chin. Lower it. Close her eyes. Smile. Frown. Laugh. In between there were Pete's lower-toned but just as insistent commands. She moved like an automaton, doing as they asked because that seemed easier than protesting. Only one command made her pause.

"Unbutton your blouse," Beau ordered.

"Huh?"

"Unbutton it."

Outrage sent Caitlin scrambling to her feet. "You're out of your mind!"

"I'm not asking you to take it off."

"I don't care."

Afterward Beau wondered how he could have done what he did next. True, he didn't have the time to spend in coaxing Caitlin. If these shots were what he wanted, he had to show them to Richter today. If not, he had to fly to Atlanta and look for another model. But he could have managed without the shot he had in mind. He didn't have to stalk over to her and unbutton her blouse himself. He undid just a few buttons, the top three, which hardly made a difference in her prim and proper blouse. However, the action was intimate and unnecessary.

But he enjoyed it. Immensely.

Only shock kept Caitlin from slapping him. Shock and the curiously weak feeling that claimed her when his hands touched her blouse. Those strong, warm hands lingered at the third button, and she stared up at him, surprised by the heat in his gaze. Was this the same man who had been yelling instructions at her for half an hour? She sucked in her breath, pulled away and slid back down on the bench. Slid, because that was the only way her suddenly liquid bones could behave. But still Beau held her gaze.

If Pete hadn't coughed, Caitlin thought she and Beau might have been frozen in this position forever. But the reminder that there were others in the room jolted them into action. Beau went back to barking orders. She went back to obeying them. The only difference was the hot, uncomfortable feeling she got when she thought of his hands on her.

Just when Caitlin had decided they had taken enough pictures to paper an entire room, Beau received a phone call, and Pete called a halt to the session.

"You're a natural," he told her as he hurried toward the darkroom. "You take direction well."

Was she supposed to be proud of that? Caitlin wondered. She gave the man a weak smile and dashed behind the curtain. She wanted out of here. Now. Before Beau could say anything more to her. Not even bothering to subdue her flyaway hair, she grabbed her purse and her glasses, waved to Brenda and sprinted for the door.

"Caitlin!" Beau's voice caught her when she was halfway to her goal. She paused in midstride and only reluctantly turned to face him.

Perched on a corner of a desk, he had placed a hand over the mouthpiece of the receiver he still held to his ear. "I want to thank you," he told her.

She nodded and turned to go, but his voice stopped her again.

"If these photographs work, I'll want you to do those ads we talked about."

She opened her mouth to protest, but no sound came out. Until this moment she had forgotten the real reason she had been photographed today. He was going to show these pictures to that important client of his. Caitlin didn't really believe the photos would work out. But on the off-chance that they did, what was she going to do? She wasn't a model. She didn't want to work with the disturbing Mr. Collins. She had enough problems already.

Her brain was formulating a protest when he suddenly barked into the phone, "How the hell did that happen?" He held up a hand, obviously an indication that Caitlin should wait until he finished his conversation, but she hurried away.

She almost ran to her car, telling herself the photographs wouldn't work. He would find himself another model. And they would pass in the hall outside their apartments just like any other two neighbors. All very safe and unexciting, very much like the rest of

Caitlin's life. That was what she wanted. Or so she told herself all the way home. Then she admitted the truth—what she really wanted from Beau Collins had nothing whatsoever to do with being safe.

Some people charted their fortune in the stars. Others looked to tea leaves for guidance. Beau Collins relied on instinct. If something was really right, he could feel it inside. And he knew the pictures of Caitlin were right. Because when he saw them, a Fourth-of-July fireworks display went off in his gut.

Beau wasn't sure they should be classified as mere photographs. Simple paper wasn't supposed to smolder as these sheets did. As he had suspected, the camera loved her face. It had captured all the hostility she had projected toward him and transformed it into a subtle sensuality. Her tangled hair and fiery eyes were balanced by her soft, vulnerable mouth and simple cotton blouse. And Beau's first impression had been right: she bore more than a passing resemblance to the fictitious Scarlett O'Hara—every inch a lady, with a vixen lurking just beneath the surface.

And that was exactly the look Dalton Richter had said he wanted for the next Plantation House Resort ad campaign. With Caitlin's photographs Beau thought he could finally deliver what Richter had in mind.

Late Saturday afternoon Beau thumbed through the photographs again as he waited patiently in Richter's outer office. It didn't do any good to get anxious. The man liked to keep people waiting in much the same way he preferred to work on weekends and call his employees in for late-night work sessions. Dalton

Richter was a difficult man, but he felt he had earned the right to run his business his own way.

Twenty-five years ago he had started with a run-down hotel in the resort town of Gatlinburg, Tennessee, not far from Knoxville. Since then he had turned that establishment around, bought similar failing hotels throughout the Southeast, and developed several new resorts.

Though no one was sure why, Richter fancied himself a Southern gentleman of old. Genuine Southern hospitality was the philosophy on which he had built his hotels and resorts. He personally saw to it that every aspect of his business—including the advertising—adhered to a certain image. And he had no use for Yankees—unless they were paying guests. Rumor had it that Richter had fired two Atlanta ad agencies in the past year because he didn't like the accents of the executives assigned to his account.

Maybe the accent was why he seemed to like Beau. Or perhaps it was just Beau's name he liked. Beauregard Perris Collins IV evoked thoughts of magnolia blossoms, cotton fields and old money. All of those could be found in Beau's ancestral past, but his branch of the family actually sprang from a black-sheep riverboat gambler who had settled in Chattanooga and invested his ill-gotten gains in several local industries. That particular ancestor was never mentioned by anyone in the family except Beau, and he talked of him often, to his mother's profound dismay. Dalton Richter, in particular, had enjoyed hearing the tale. Beau thought it ironic that the only family member to ever help him in business was a renegade gambler much like himself.

He was thinking about that ancestor when Richter at last emerged from his inner office. As usual the older man was dressed in a suit that matched his hair in snowy whiteness, and he was waving a cigar and blustering to some hapless employee about something. His pontificating ended when he caught sight of Beau. With a grateful glance, the employee escaped while Richter advanced on his new target.

"Beau, my boy! Good to see you." His handshake was hearty, and his booming laughter rattled the glass in the room's expansive window.

"I hope you've got something better to show me this time," Richter continued, not giving Beau a chance to reply. "We've got to make some decisions, you know."

"Yes, sir. I know that." Beau knew that very well. Friendly and amiable though Richter had been until now, he had given Beau a deadline of this coming Tuesday to find the right model for the proposed campaign. Finding the perfect face was the first part of a test. The campaign was the next part. If Beau passed, his agency would have won Richter's trust. That translated into big bucks.

Squaring his shoulders, Beau followed Richter into his office, waited until the man was seated and then spread four of the best photographs of Caitlin across the smooth surface of the desk. No explanation was necessary. The photos spoke for themselves. In them, Caitlin progressed from an almost demure hand-to-cheek pose to blouse-unbuttoned desirability.

"Great balls of fire," Richter bellowed, his eyes bulging in appreciation. "Now you've got somethin', Collins."

"I knew you'd be pleased."

"I just wanna know when I can meet her."

Beau politely joined in the conspiratorial masculine laughter, but he faltered for a moment, thinking of the way Caitlin had looked before the pictures were taken. But he wasn't going to borrow trouble. If Richter wanted to meet her, he'd think of something. He always did.

Richter slapped the top of the desk. "Okay, Collins, we're in business. I've got big plans."

He wanted full-color brochures on his hotels in Hilton Head, Savannah, New Orleans and Atlanta. Color advertisements on each of those same hotels, placed in all the major travel magazines as well as the publications put out by state tourist bureaus. Black-and-white ads in newspapers. Two more Plantation House Resorts were scheduled to open in Florida and Alabama during the next year, and he'd want to make a big splash about them, too.

The plans were exactly what Beau had suggested when he had first met with Richter. However, he had never expected the man to take all his suggestions. An adman always asked for more than he hoped to get. But for all Richter's eccentricity, it seemed at base he was a shrewd man, and he wanted a bigger piece of the resort-industry pie. A stepped-up advertising program could put him closer to his goal.

The older man winked, and his words were an echo of what Beau had said to him in an earlier meeting. "If I'm gonna play with the big boys, I've gotta get my name out there, don't I?"

"Absolutely," Beau agreed, pretending he had never heard the words before.

Richter leaned back in his chair and puffed contentedly on his cigar. "You know, son, if you handle this right, you and I could be doing business for a long, long time."

The words were music to Beau's ears. This was exactly what he needed. With a stable, long-term client as a base, his agency could do nothing but grow. This campaign was going to be handled just as Richter wanted. He'd make sure of that.

Richter took him to dinner. They imbibed the accepted quota of Jack Daniel's and talked until late in the evening about costs and timetables and logistics. Beau was so pumped up and enthused that he forgot one tiny detail. The tiny detail upon which the entire project hinged.

*Caitlin had never promised to do the ads.*

He remembered about five-thirty the next morning, and he sat straight up in bed. Why hadn't he got this straight with Caitlin? At the studio he had gotten that phone call—the wrong radio spots were running for another client in Chattanooga—and he asked Caitlin to wait. She hadn't. He had had to make several more calls to straighten out the radio crisis. Then Pete had started printing the shots of Caitlin. Not another thought had been spared for getting her promise.

Beau muttered a curse in the darkness, tossed back the covers and swung his legs to the floor. What an aggravation. Not that convincing Caitlin should be that big a problem. Who would pass up a chance like this? Especially after he showed her those pictures. She'd have to like the way she looked. Any woman would.

But that was exactly the problem, he decided, rubbing a hand along his unshaven jaw. Caitlin didn't seem like most of the women he knew. She had none of the feminine guile or flirtatious pretense he was used to. She was genuine. Everything she felt showed on her face. In their short acquaintance she had run the gamut of feelings from fear to outrage to amusement to desire to...

Desire. Beau paused there, his thoughts taking him back to that moment when he had unbuttoned Caitlin's blouse. She hadn't stopped him. She had just gazed at him with those big, innocent hazel eyes. Eyes that could hypnotize a man.

"Damn!" All hope of sleep gone, he jumped up from the bed, pulled on a pair of jeans and went to the kitchen. His cupboards contained nothing but a can of coffee, his refrigerator held only four slices of three-day-old pizza, two beers and a bottle of champagne.

"Coffee and pizza, my favorite breakfast," he murmured. He would eat, take a shower and then work out some details of what he and Richter had discussed last night. He'd keep his thoughts off Caitlin Welch. At a decent hour, he would simply knock on her door and convince her to do the ads. No fuss. No problem. He could handle it.

Perhaps if the pizza had been fresher or the coffee stronger, Beau's plan might have worked. As it was, however, he kept glancing at Caitlin's photograph. She looked both saint and sinner. Incredibly sexy. He wondered which side of her would rule when she was in bed with a man. *In bed with him.* That thought signaled the end of any pretense of working. He was soon knocking on her door—a full hour ahead of when he'd planned to approach her.

Caitlin had been expecting a knock. But she hadn't expected Beau Collins. After spending all last night convincing herself that she didn't want anything to do with him, her first impulse was to close the door in his face. That idea was ruined, however, because her mother also chose that exact moment to appear.

"My, my," Beverly Welch murmured in the husky voice her daughter loved so well. Her warm brown eyes traveled over Beau with interest, and the tiniest of smiles touched her mouth. "Are we having a guest for brunch?"

"Yes, you are," Beau interjected before Caitlin could protest. "I was just going back to my apartment to get the champagne."

"Champagne?" Caitlin managed to choke out as he disappeared into his apartment.

"You could have told me, Caitlin," her mother stage-whispered. The gleam in her eyes was decidedly wicked. "I'd have brought a date of my own."

Later, Caitlin stood fuming in the kitchen as she prepared to scramble some eggs. A burst of laughter from the living room drowned out the sizzle of frying bacon, and she dropped an eggshell in the bowl.

"Mother needs a little more orange juice added to that champagne," she muttered, fishing the shell out with a fork. She added milk and cheese, uncaring of the amounts. Her mother usually fixed the eggs during their weekly Sunday brunches. Today, however, she was too busy being charmed by Beau Collins. What were they talking about in there?

Damn him, anyway, Caitlin thought, plucking the bacon from the skillet to drain. He shouldn't even be here. Yesterday should have been the end of it. The photos should have proved she wasn't a model. He should go away instead of inviting himself to brunch, flirting with her mother and sending tingles up and down Caitlin's spine with that smile of his.

Without ceremony, she dumped the eggs in the skillet, turned up the temperature and leaned down to get the croissants out of the oven. As she was pulling the tray out, her mother gave an odd little shriek and called her name. Caitlin jumped, the oven door slammed, and the tray teetered dangerously before she dropped it to the stove top. Pulling off her oven mitts, she stalked to the doorway.

"Mother, for heaven's sake," she began, but the words died in her throat when she saw what awaited her.

Pictures were lined up on the couch, on the chairs and across the shelf over her television set. Color pictures. Eight by tens. In full living color. About twenty pictures of her. Or at least someone who looked like her. Vaguely. No one spoke while her gaze spun from photo to photo and back again. It couldn't be. It just couldn't.

"Caitlin, why didn't you tell me about this?" her mother demanded at last.

She merely shook her head and looked at Beau. He wore a smug smile.

"I knew you could do it," he said. "The client loved you. I want you to pose for those ads."

Feeling as if the air had been sucked from her lungs, Caitlin continued to stare at him.

"What ads?" her mother asked.

"Plantation House Resorts, an account of mine," Beau answered her, though his gaze was on Caitlin. He stepped toward her. "You will do it, won't you?"

Still rooted to the spot, she found her voice. "No."

Beverly Welch's soft sigh was full of disappointment. "Oh, Caitlin, why?"

"Because it's not me. It's not . . ." Caitlin faltered, not knowing how to explain how she felt. A person could go through her whole life wishing to be transformed into someone glamorous and different and exciting. Yet when the miracle happened, when confronted with the change, as she was confronted with these startling pictures, then it was almost too much. The person in those photographs was an unknown quantity. Caitlin couldn't be that person. She wouldn't know how to think or act or feel.

Trying to explain that to the two handsome people in front of her was an impossible task. As swans, how could they possibly understand an ugly duckling's fears?

Thankfully, the smell of burning eggs reached the living room before Caitlin had to attempt any further explanation. The kitchen's smoke alarm buzzed at the same time, and several minutes were occupied by opening windows, shutting off the alarm and scraping the charred mess out of the skillet. By the time the crisis was over, her mother was looking at her with the stubborn, don't-argue-with-me expression Caitlin knew only too well. No one could dissuade Beverly Welch when she looked like this.

"I'd like to hear exactly what Beau is proposing with these ads," she said. "I don't think you should make any rash decisions before you know the whole story, Caitlin."

"Mother, I don't—"

Beverly pushed her toward the table in the corner of the kitchen. "Sit down. We'll all have some breakfast and talk."

"Breakfast is ruined, and—"

"Stop making excuses and sit down," Beverly ordered.

Knowing it was useless to argue, Caitlin sat down, poured herself a cup of coffee and tried to block Beau out her line of vision, no easy feat in her small kitchen.

Beau had been hovering in the doorway, amused by the exchange between mother and daughter. Beverly Welch was his kind of woman. He had recognized a kindred spirit the moment he met her. With any luck she was going to win him her daughter's cooperation.

Beverly turned to him, still speaking in the no-nonsense tones only a mother can perfect. "I want you to sit down, too. And start explaining about these ads."

He followed orders, taking a seat across from Caitlin and filling Beverly in on Dalton Richter's *Gone With the Wind* preoccupation. He left out the exact way he had met her daughter, but he detailed yesterday's photo session and Richter's reaction.

"Everything's set," he said as Beverly placed a cheese-and-bacon croissant sandwich in front of him. "If I can get your daughter's cooperation, that is." Caitlin glared at him.

"What's all set?" Beverly asked, taking a seat, too. "What kind of ads are these going to be?"

As they ate he explained the planned design of the advertisements, his enthusiasm making him forget everything but how excited he was about this campaign. The black-and-white background would feature Caitlin, dressed in full antebellum costume. Clustered in the foreground would be smaller color photographs of her at the various resorts—golfing, playing tennis, swimming, dining, dancing—whatever shots worked out the best. They'd show the consummate southern belle, then and now. "The caption is simple—'The charm of the Old South lives on today at Plantation House.'" He paused and looked expectantly at the two women. "What do you think?"

"I like it," Beverly said without hesitation.

Caitlin was pointedly silent, her expression baleful.

Ignoring her, Beau continued. "We'll do brochures that follow the same basic theme for all four hotels and resorts."

"Four?" Beverly asked.

Beau nodded. "Hilton Head, Savannah, New Orleans and Atlanta." He wasn't mentioning next year's Jacksonville, Florida and Mobile, Alabama just yet. Why push his luck?

"Will Caitlin have to go to all the resorts?"

"Of course. I expect the whole project to take a couple of weeks. Richter is providing his private plane, and he's promised VIP treatment for the photography crew and Caitlin at the resorts. Caitlin won't be working every minute, so she can make a vacation of it."

"How much are you going to pay her?"

He named a sum that made Beverly's eyes widen.

She set her coffee cup down with a clatter and turned to her daughter. "I think you should do it."

"Mother, please." Caitlin protested. "I can't do something like this."

"And why not?"

"Because I'm not a model."

"No," Beau cut in, "but those pictures in the other room show that you could be."

She had no answer for that but her jaw remained set in a stubborn line as she glared at her two companions.

Beau knew when to stop pushing. If he stayed any longer he was going to make Caitlin so furious she'd probably never agree to the job. He was going to put the rest of this argument in her mother's capable hands.

He pushed away from the table and stood. "I'm going to leave you alone to think about this, but I need to know something tonight." He started for the door and then turned around. "I hope you decide to do it," he said softly, capturing Caitlin's gaze with his own. "Who knows? You might even have some fun." With a smile and wave he was gone.

"Caitlin . . ." her mother began as soon as the front door clicked shut.

She got up and started clearing the table. "Mother, don't start with me."

"But how can you think of *not* doing this?"

"Easy."

Beverly was silent for a moment while Caitlin rattled dishes in the sink. "He's right, you know," she said softly.

Caitlin eyed her with suspicion. "Right about what?"

"About having some fun."

"What does that have to do with anything?"

"When was the last time you had any fun?" her mother pressed.

"Mother—"

"Too long ago to remember?"

"Don't be silly," Caitlin snapped.

"You're the one who is being silly," Beverly countered. She stood and took hold of her daughter's arm. "Come here."

Caitlin allowed herself to be pulled into the living room where the disturbing pictures still stared back at her.

"These are so gorgeous," her mother murmured. "Aren't you excited to see yourself this way?"

"No," Caitlin replied, only to realize she was lying. It was a little exciting to discover the woman in these pictures, stranger though she was, lurked somewhere inside her. She swallowed. "I mean... they're exciting, I guess, but they're so... unexpected."

"I don't know why," her mother murmured. "I always said you had a pretty face. But you were always hiding behind those unnecessary glasses and pretending you didn't care how you looked."

Caitlin smiled at the familiar words. For as long as she could remember, her mother had been telling her what a pretty girl she could be if she'd just stand up straight or stop scowling or cut her hair or get contact lenses. Beverly herself was a lovely woman. Even now, after all the years of struggling to raise her two children alone, she had a special kind of glow. Her eyes were bright with good humor, her dark hair softly styled, her figure still trim. She wasn't a vain person, but appearances were important to her. Perhaps that was why Caitlin had always worked so hard to not be attractive. That small rebellion had been the only aberration in an otherwise obedient child. And as she had grown older, not caring about her looks had become a habit.

Beverly reached out and touched her daughter's hair. "Everyone used to tell me how lucky I was to have such a good child," she murmured. "And I used to think it might not be so bad if you'd misbehave a little more."

"I wish I'd known that," Caitlin quipped. "I'd have broken a few more dishes."

"No you wouldn't have." Beverly moved away and picked up one of the photographs. "When there's a child in the family who is special in the way that Julie was, it puts a strain on everyone else. I used to think the strain was hardest on your father. After all, Julie was why he left..." Her voice trailed away as she stood looking down at a picture.

Caitlin joined her, placing a hand on her mother's arm. Her father was a subject they rarely discussed.

Beverly patted her hand and continued. "Now I think it was you who suffered the most because of Julie."

"Mother, I loved her. I would have done anything—"

"That's what I mean," Beverly interrupted. "You do everything for everyone else. For Julie. For me. For your students. For that stupid Tom Leland who decided a job in California was more important than you were. It's time you did something for yourself."

"Maybe so," Caitlin agreed. "But running off to pose for a bunch of ads isn't what I need."

"Why not? You've got nearly all summer to do something different." Beverly tapped the photograph she still held. "Do something you never expected to do, Caitlin. Have some fun."

Caitlin hated to admit it, but there was a certain appeal in what her mother said. Reluctantly, she agreed to at least consider Beau Collins's offer, and

Beverly didn't mention it again. She hugged her daughter and left. And Caitlin sat down to think.

It wasn't that she was afraid to do this. What was there to frighten her? Yesterday's photo session might have been fun if it hadn't been for Beau. Caitlin shivered, remembering Beau, remembering his hands in her hair and at the buttons of her blouse. Maybe he was the real reason she hesitated. Doing this job would probably mean being with him, and she didn't know if that was wise. He was a swan, and despite what the photographs of her said, Caitlin wasn't. There couldn't be anything between them.

The day wore on, and she paced her apartment, feeling hemmed in by the familiar walls, wondering if she could face a summer of this sameness. The heat brewed an early evening thunderstorm. Seated in the middle of her living-room rug, still thinking, Caitlin felt the storm building. She watched the room darken, heard the approaching rumbles of thunder. Lightning flashed, playing across her pictures. The effect was eerie, but it seemed to underline her restlessness.

What did she want, anyway? A particularly loud clap of thunder jolted her, and the answer was suddenly as clear as the lightning that followed.

Quickly, before she could reconsider, she crossed the hall to Beau's apartment and pushed the doorbell. Nothing happened, and she at first knocked and then banged on the door. It was flung open before she could knock again, and he stood, shirtless, his hair tousled, blinking at her as if he'd just been roused from a deep sleep.

"Caitlin?" he whispered.

She swallowed. What she had planned to say had been erased by the unexpected sight of his muscular chest and the fine line of sun-kissed hair that angled downward to his unsnapped jeans. Beyond that point Caitlin couldn't let her eyes wander. She looked up and into his eyes instead.

Outside, the rain had begun. A cloudburst beat against the porch roof and the front door blew open, but neither she nor Beau made a move to close it. Caitlin drew in a deep breath of the sweet rain air and tried to remember what she had wanted to tell him.

"Caitlin?" he said again, taking a step forward.

She found her voice then, though it was an effort. "I'll do it," she whispered.

Behind her, the front door banged against the wall. Wide open to the storm.

## *Chapter Three*

With an appreciative sigh, Beau settled back against soft leather cushions. No airplane seat had ever felt this good, but of course he hadn't spent much time on board private jets. Perhaps they were all this luxurious. Or perhaps Dalton Richter's plane was an exception, another expression of the man's flamboyant style.

The plane's cabin was compact but beautifully appointed. Brocade curtains were tied back from the windows. Plush carpet cushioned the walls and floor, and a fully stocked bar ran the width of the plane behind the passenger seats. Beau could see that his assistant, Molly Peters, was already taking advantage of the broad seats to spread out some of her ever-present paperwork. Pete and Brenda had settled into the seats facing her. Everyone seemed ready to enjoy their luxurious surroundings on the short trip to Savannah, Georgia.

"This is the life, isn't it?" Beau murmured, turning to the woman seated beside him.

To his surprise Caitlin looked anything but relaxed. Her face was pale, and she was holding on to the burgundy leather armrests as if she feared she'd be ejected from the plane at any moment. Beau covered her hand with his own. "Are you okay?"

The muscles in her throat worked convulsively as she stared at him, her frightened eyes more green than hazel.

"You look like you've never been on a plane before," he teased. He frowned when she still didn't speak. "Are you saying you've never flown before?" She nodded and clutched tightly at his hand. "It's going to be fine," he whispered, but the words were drowned out by the escalating roar of the engines.

Appearing more frightened than ever, Caitlin squeezed her eyes shut while the plane taxied to the runway and prepared for takeoff. Her hand was still firmly held in his. Beau decided he rather liked the sensation of comforting the elusive Miss Caitlin Welch.

She'd had little to say to him since last Sunday evening when she had come to his door and agreed to his offer. In fact, she had run away like a scared rabbit that day. On Monday she had signed the contract and disappeared. The rest of the week she had spent with Molly, shopping for a wardrobe. Friday night there had been a dinner at Dalton Richter's home, and he had monopolized Caitlin's attention. She had laughed at his outlandish stories. He had seemed captivated.

Beau couldn't blame the man; Caitlin had looked gorgeous that night. She had left her glasses behind in favor of contact lenses. Brenda had done her hair and makeup. Molly had put her in one of the dresses purchased for the shoot. Though the dress had been bright red in color, its style had been rather conservative. Caitlin had probably thought she looked suitably demure. But Beau could still remember the flirtatious way the hem had danced about her shapely legs. She had great legs, the kind that seemed to go on forever, the kind a man liked to imagine entwined with his own.

Beau looked down, hoping for a glimpse of those legs now, but there was little to see. Her neat beige skirt effectively covered her knees. He sighed in disappointment. A woman with legs like hers should show them off at every opportunity. He glanced back at her face. At least she had left her glasses off and was wearing some makeup, even if her gorgeous hair was skimmed back in its habitual bun.

The plane started down the runway, and she opened terror-filled eyes. Beau smiled at her. "There's nothing to this. Just sit back and enjoy the ride."

"You must think I'm an idiot," she managed to say.

"Not at all. Just hold on to me. I've always been good with virg..." he paused and winked at her, "uh...I mean first-time flyers."

His teasing tone and choice of words were clearly not lost on Caitlin. Terror forgotten, she snatched her hand away. Color tinted her cheeks, and she turned to gaze out the window as the plane lifted into the air.

Beau bit back a laugh. For all he knew Caitlin was a virgin in more ways than one. That seemed improbable in this day and age, but she did have an untouched air about her. Untouched? He studied her stiffly averted figure for a moment. No, maybe the correct term was unexplored. He sensed there was passion in Caitlin's depths, passion he'd lay odds no man had ever bothered to investigate. Whatever the case, she wasn't like any other woman he'd ever known.

Of course most women of his acquaintance were of a particular type. Mostly blondes. Tall and voluptuous and self-possessed, undemanding of anything more than a good time. They were the kind of women his mother usually felt were most inappropriate for a *Collins* to be dating. Of course that was exactly the reason Beau had dated many of them. When he was younger, he had enjoyed bringing his more flamboyant girlfriends to dinner at the family home. His mother had always been coolly, distantly polite. Nothing could crack that genteel facade of hers, but it had pleased Beau to know she was cringing inside. After such an evening, there would always be a phone call from his father, a reprimand, an inquiry into the seriousness of Beau's relationship with his unsuitable date. On occasion he had made his father squirm a little by pretending a serious interest where there had been none.

Beau still chose undemanding women. The only commitment he had time for was his advertising agency. But as for shocking his parents—he no longer cared. The only person in his family with whom he was in regular contact was his cousin Melissa.

That wasn't entirely true, he admitted reluctantly. His father had called several times in the last few weeks, urging him to come for a visit when he was in Chattanooga. Beau had brushed those calls aside.

What possible interest did his parents have in their son, the disappointment?

Perhaps his father had gotten wind of his business problems and wanted to gloat. Beau's gut twisted at the thought. Four years ago when he had opened his agency, he had asked his father for financial backing. In his adult life that was the only favor he had asked of his father. Beau had actually thought the man would like to see his son running a company of his own. He should have known better. As usual, what his son wanted or thought had made little impression on Perry Collins. He had laughed and predicted failure. Beau had resolved then to prove him wrong. He had started his business without his father's help. And he'd damn well hold on to it without his help.

That was exactly why Beau was going to supervise the Plantation House Resort shoot himself. Normally, he would have placed the project in the capable hands of Pete and Molly or the agency's art director. But too much was riding on this account. If something went wrong, he wanted to know it was no one's fault but his own. His qualified staff would deal with the rest of the agency's business for now.

The pilot's announcement that they had reached cruising altitude broke into Beau's thoughts. Beside him Caitlin stirred in her seat, her body seeming to relax. "Feeling better?" he asked.

"Yes, thank you." Her tone was cold and stiff, making Beau grin. She bristled, and his smile broadened. He liked her when she was angry with him.

"What's the matter?" Pete called from across the aisle. "Caitlin afraid of flying?"

"A little. But I think she's okay now." With gentle fingers Beau lifted her chin, his gaze capturing hers. "You are okay, aren't you?"

Caitlin shivered at his touch, and her irritation vanished under his concerned regard. She lost all sense of herself when she looked into his eyes. Looking at him was how she had ended up on this plane. Last Sunday night she should have called him and said no, instead of charging across the hall, being confronted with his sleepy eyes and bare chest and saying yes. A hundred times since then she had wanted to call the whole thing off, but under his warm gaze she had signed the contracts and committed herself to this crazy adventure. Since then she had successfully avoided him until they boarded this plane at the Knoxville airport. It was just her luck he had chosen to sit beside her.

"Caitlin?" he murmured, and as usual his accent softened, sweetened her name. When he spoke to her like that, it was easy to imagine he might actually be interested in her. Even without the sound of his voice, she had imagined the same thing throughout the past week.

Annoyed by that fanciful thought, Caitlin swallowed. "I'm fine."

His knuckles stroked across the curve of her cheek before his hand fell away from her face. "Good. I always like coming to the aid of a damsel in distress."

Laughter erupted from the other occupants of the plane, and Caitlin looked up, certain they had been taking in her exchange with Beau. To her relief, however, Molly was telling the others something about Dalton Richter.

"What's up?" Beau asked.

Pete explained. "Is that true that Richter won this plane in a poker game?"

"I wouldn't doubt it."

"Well, I'm going to get him to give me some lessons at the game," Brenda declared.

Shaking his head, Pete patted his wife's hand. "Now, honey, you know you just don't have a gambler's instinct." To the others he explained, "She spent our entire honeymoon cruise playing blackjack. We were flat busted at the end of the trip."

Brenda tossed her head. "Well, if you hadn't spent the whole cruise in your bed, seasick . . ."

A chorus of catcalls from Beau and Molly greeted this last statement, and Pete endured some good-natured ribbing about spending his honeymoon in bed alone.

While the others talked and laughed, Caitlin sat silently beside Beau. How foolish of her to think for even a minute that he had anything other than a professional interest in her. That he teased her and held her hand proved nothing. He acted the same way with everyone.

Caitlin pretended to bury her nose in a book, but in reality she watched as Beau teased Molly about her new short-cropped hairdo. He had moved over behind his assistant's seat and was touching her hair and grinning down at her in that flirtatious way of his. Caitlin swallowed hard, remembering his hands in her own hair. Firmly, she went back to her book, but another burst of laughter drew her gaze back to Beau and Molly.

She wasn't jealous. Caitlin had spent enough time with Molly this week to know there was nothing between her and Beau. Molly was even-tempered and pretty, and Beau had said his entire business would come unglued without her. They were friends, but the relationship was mainly professional. On Molly's left hand was a diamond engagement ring, and she was planning a September wedding to her college sweetheart.

Caitlin watched the fresh-faced brunette giggle up at Beau. She envied the ease with which Molly laughed off his attention. The same attention—teasing or not—would have reduced Caitlin to a quivering mass of nerves.

No one else seemed to have her problem. Beau flirted outrageously with the woman who picked them up at the Savannah airport in a Plantation House Resort van. She flirted right back, all during the hour-long drive north to Hilton Head Island. And when they arrived at the resort, Beau transferred his charming attention to the attractive assistant manager who gave them a brief tour on the way to Dalton Richter's private three-bedroom condominium.

The resort was beautiful. It consisted of a five-story hotel on the beach, a charming village of time-share condos, two pools, tennis courts, a golf course, a glass-domed clubhouse and an open-air pavilion restaurant with room for dancing at night. Flowers scented the air, and ancient oaks shaded the path to the condo.

While the others oohed and ahhed over their luxurious accomodations, Caitlin heard Beau make a date to meet the manager later. Again berating herself for her silly romantic thoughts about him, she picked up her carry-on case and followed Molly upstairs. Almost immediately Beau was beside her, taking the bag out of her hand.

On the landing he flashed both women a smile. "I hope you two don't mind sharing a room."

The room in question was huge. Blue silk comforters covered two double beds, and matching draperies framed a spectacular ocean view. Through an open door Caitlin glimpsed a blue-and-white bath.

Molly gave one of the beds an experimental bounce. "I think Caitlin and I can suffer through a few days in here."

"Are you sure?" Beau pressed. "Because if not, one of you can bunk in with me. I think I've only got one bed, but we'll make do somehow." Grasping Caitlin's elbow, he tugged her toward the door. "Come on, I'll put your stuff in my room."

Caitlin could feel the now-familiar flush creeping into her cheeks, even as she attempted a stiff little smile. What was wrong with her? There was no reason to get all hot and bothered. He was only kidding. Thankfully, Molly's laughter kept the moment from becoming awkward.

"Put her bag down and get out of here," she ordered, practically pushing Beau from the room before she closed the door behind him. Still laughing, she lifted her suitcase to the bed. "Don't let him get to you, Caitlin."

"Oh, I won't," Caitlin replied, wishing she felt as confident as her words implied.

"Tomorrow he'll be all business, and you'll wish he would tease you a little."

"I doubt it." Opening her own suitcase, Caitlin began putting clothes in the closet and the bureau drawers.

"You must not have any brothers," Molly commented after they had worked a few minutes in companionable silence.

"Huh?"

"Any brothers?"

"No, only a sister," Caitlin replied. Thinking of Julie still brought the usual tug of sadness.

"I figured as much." Molly pushed a bureau drawer shut with her hip and smiled. "If you had brothers, you'd know how to take the kidding. I have four of 'em, all older, and I learned real early how to handle wise guys like Beau."

Caitlin didn't think a dozen brothers would help her cope with the way Beau disturbed her. There was nothing sisterly in the feelings his teasing aroused. But not for anything would she reveal those feelings, even to someone as nice as Molly. "I guess I just don't expect him to act the way he does." At the other woman's raised eyebrow, she defended herself, "After all, he is the boss."

"I think that's why everyone at the agency likes working for him," Molly replied, pausing in the bathroom doorway with swimsuit in hand. "Most of the time he doesn't act like a boss."

"Most of the time?"

"Let's just say he's had his bad moments during the past year."

"Why?"

"Just a couple of tough breaks," she murmured evasively before closing the door and the subject. "Come on," she called from inside the bathroom, "let's head for the beach. There's still a couple of hours of sun, and we don't have to work until tomorrow."

Caitlin spared little time worrying about whatever bad breaks had befallen Beau. He appeared to be the kind of man who could land on his feet, and there were other things to occupy her attention—like the inordinate amount of skin her new swimsuit revealed.

"Whoa," Molly said, coming out of the bathroom in her own conservative blue maillot. "That is some swimsuit."

"It didn't look so bad on the hanger." Caitlin groaned and frowned at her reflection in the mirror. The suit was bright red in color, cut high on the legs and slashed almost to the waist in the front. Her mother had insisted on buying it, along with several other outfits now hanging in the closet. Caitlin had spent so much time trying on clothes with Molly this past week that she had simply relied on her mother's judgment for a few personal purchases. Clearly a mistake, she told herself, grimacing into the mirror.

Molly giggled. "At least you won't have to worry too much about tan lines." She slipped into a cover-up and stuffed a towel and suntan lotion into a canvas bag.

"Maybe it's the wrong size," Caitlin muttered, attempting to tug her suit into a semblance of modesty.

A knock at the door cut off Molly's reply, and Beau came in before Caitlin could react.

"I just wanted to let you know when we're going to meet for din..." His voice trailed away in midword as soon as he noticed Caitlin. She resisted the impulse to pull at her suit again, knowing that would only make the situation worse.

He let go with a long, appreciative whistle. "Wow. Did you pick this out, Molly?"

"I know my job better than that," she declared, pretending to be insulted. "The suits she'll wear in the ads are very modest. These are family resorts, after all."

"A pity," Beau murmured, continuing to give Caitlin an admiring assessment while Molly chattered on about the clothes she had selected for the shoot.

Caitlin reached for her beach jacket, hoping her embarrassment wasn't too obvious. Beau probably thought her completely lacking in sophistication. Until today she'd never flown on a plane. She didn't know how to flirt. And she most certainly didn't know how to deal with the interest her skimpy attire had sparked in his green eyes. She almost dropped her jacket as he continued to gaze at her.

Amused, Beau watched her futile attempts to get into the cover-up. Most women wouldn't mind being admired by a man, but the fact that Caitlin wasn't just any woman had already been established. He imagined she didn't know how alluring she looked. And she was alluring. If the tightening of his body was any way to judge, she could be called downright arousing.

She didn't exactly have a healthy tan. But there was something very sexy about the creamy glow of her skin against the ruby-red material of her swimsuit. That skin was as inviting to the touch as the delicate inner folds of a seashell.

The invitation was more tempting than stronger men could have resisted. And Beau had never admitted to any strength where the fair sex was concerned. Pushing her fumbling hands aside, he settled the jacket across her shoulders. In doing so his, fingers skimmed her smooth, warm skin. So smooth. So warm. The sort of skin that encouraged a man to linger, to savor. Would she taste as delicious as she felt?

That question sent erotic images exploding through his head. A simple touch wasn't supposed to cause such a reaction. Startled, Beau's glance clashed with Caitlin's. Her eyes were wide, a little puzzled, very vulnerable. Did she guess what he was thinking? What would she say if he told her he wanted to kiss the tiny pulse that was beating at her throat? What if he pressed his mouth between the soft swells of her breasts?

Even as that appealing thought went through his mind, she was shrugging off his hands and sliding her arms into her jacket. Beau swallowed and took a step backward, suddenly realizing that Molly had stopped talking. Hands on hips, she was regarding him with a narrowed, suspicious glance. He avoided her eyes and cleared his throat.

Caitlin broke the silence by murmuring something about contact lenses and retreating behind a closed bathroom door.

Molly's whisper had a sharp edge. "I know that look in your eyes, Beau Collins, and I don't think she's your kind at all."

He managed to laugh. "Don't worry, mother hen. She's not." On the way out the door, he patted her shoulder. "We'll meet for dinner in the pavilion at seven-thirty, okay?"

"Beau, come back here and promise me..."

His assistant's voice faded as Beau hurried from the room and downstairs. He didn't have time to listen to any lectures. With the manager's help, they were going to scout locations for tomorrow's work. He didn't have time to think about anything but this ad campaign.

But the memory of Caitlin's soft skin lingered. Intruded. Marred his concentration. By the afternoon's end he was leaving all the decisions up to Pete. By evening he was impatiently waiting to see her at dinner.

She's a witch, he decided as she slid into a seat across the dinner table. Or a chameleon. Maybe both. Every time he saw her, she seemed to have changed. And the difference went deeper than clothes or hairstyle or makeup.

The physical changes were all part of it, yes, but not all. Tonight she bore little superficial resemblance to the buttoned-up prude who had appeared at Pete's studio a week ago. Her simple sundress was white, flattering to skin that was rosy from an afternoon at the beach. Her hair was caught back in a bun, but the style was softer than usual. She looked . . . nice. Nothing more than nice. Although she could have looked spectacular.

What prevented that? Beau studied Caitlin all through dinner, trying to answer the question. Finally, he decided it was attitude. She always seemed to be holding herself back. Like a little girl at a grown-up party, she was intent on melting into the background, content to make no demands and cause no problems. When she forgot to hold back, when she let go with pure, unguarded feelings, then she was truly breathtaking. He'd seen flashes of those feelings—the fear when she'd confronted him with the gun, the anger at the photo session, the embarrassment when he'd surprised her in that swimsuit. But all too often she wore a carefully blank expression.

What made a person bury their emotions? A wry smile twisted his lips. He should know. He had his own disguises, and only a few people were allowed a glimpse beneath them. Melissa and Hunt. Sometimes Molly. For everyone else, especially his parents, he maintained a carefully nonchalant pose. He certainly understood the need for a mask. His ready smile served the same purpose as the serious air with which Caitlin cloaked herself.

She was definitely serious tonight, avoiding his gaze, speaking to the others only when spoken to, watching the couples in the dance pavilion without a trace of yearning. Only her hands betrayed her, her slender fingers tapping the table in perfect time with the music.

Beau grinned. He had told Caitlin that accepting this job would be fun. It could be, but first she had to let loose and enjoy herself. If she knew how. He suspected she didn't. But who better to teach her than an admitted master of the fine art of showing ladies a good time?

Grasping her hand, he pulled her to her feet. "Let's dance."

"But I can't."

Ignoring her protest he drew her onto the dance floor and into his arms. "Just relax and follow me."

The music was slow, sultry. The lyrics suggested heartbreak, but the melody was a sensual encouragement. Inspired by the beat, bodies pressed close together. Hips swayed in imitation of a movement more intimate in nature. With this music washing over them, a man and a woman needed no excuse to touch.

Or so it seemed to Caitlin. And for a few moments she closed her eyes and lost herself in a flood of sensations. The gentle brush of Beau's cotton trousers against her bare legs. The warm scent of the ocean breeze. The multicolored blur of other dancers twirling past them. How heavenly this was. To be held like this, to move like this with a man like Beau.

Beau. Remembering who held her, Caitlin opened her eyes. His were shut, and because she was so close, she could see that the lashes she had thought so dark were in reality tipped with gold. Just like the hair on his chest. Remembering his broad, bare chest made her stumble.

His eyes flew open. "Now why did you do that?"

"I told you I don't dance."

"You were doing just fine until you started thinking."

She flushed. Could he guess what she'd been thinking?

"You think too much," Beau continued. "Just go with the music." To illustrate, he took her through a series of twirls. Caitlin stumbled again.

"You see," she snapped. "I can't dance."

"Anyone can dance."

"I can't."

"Yes, you can."

Rather than argue, she gritted her teeth and concentrated on following his lead.

He studied her silently for a moment. "I imagine there's a whole list of things you can't do, isn't there?"

"And I suppose *you* can do everything?"

The challenge in her words put a twinkle in his eyes. "What do you think?"

"I think you're too sure of yourself."

"Probably. But I've never found it to be too much of a problem."

"Other people might disagree with you."

He threw back his head and laughed. "Other people's opinions have also never presented much of a problem."

The music ended before Caitlin could think of a suitable reply. She started to pull away, but he held her steady and swung her into the next dance. This time the music was a little faster, unfamiliar to her but with a definite Latin flavor. Beau seemed able to dance to anything, and her attempts to put some distance between their bodies only made him draw her tighter against him. She retaliated by holding herself as stiff as possible.

She flashed him a triumphant smile. "You might be able to make me stay on the dance floor, but you can't make me like it."

"Wanna bet?" His voice was a silken, sexy threat.

The warning that sounded in her head told her not to ask, but she couldn't resist. "And just how will you make me?"

"Like this." The words were almost lost as he pressed his lips against her neck. His mouth was warm, open, moist. She could feel the tip of his tongue trace a line from beneath her ear to the top of her shoulder.

As he had intended, Beau felt her body melt against his. But his mouth lingered against her skin. It was just as he had imagined. She tasted as delicious as she looked.

He was further rewarded when he lifted his gaze to meet hers. Fire smoldered in her eyes. A spark of excitement. She was definitely letting her emotions show. Exactly as he had intended. They swayed together, hip to hip, looking deep into each other's eyes until Beau drew her closer and laid his cheek against her hair.

"Are you enjoying yourself now?" he murmured.

There was nothing for Caitlin to do but nod. His question was rhetorical. She couldn't hide her reaction to him.

His breath was warm against her ear as he spoke. "At school we used to say you could tell a lot about a girl by the way she danced."

"Really?" Caitlin managed to whisper. That she could speak at all was a surprise.

"Yeah. Supposedly a girl who could dance was real easy."

"Was it true?" she asked automatically and right away wanted to recall the words.

He chuckled. "I don't know. I was always one for a challenge. I'd ask out the girls who couldn't dance." He drew back and brought his hand up to feather through the curling tendrils of hair that had escaped from her bun. "I guess you could say I still like a challenge."

For the first time since he'd kissed her, Caitlin's steps faltered.

"You're thinking again," Beau admonished her. "Don't think. Feel."

That was the whole problem. Her feelings were guiding her actions far too much. The memory of his mouth against her skin was preventing any logical thought. If she could just think straight for two minutes she'd find a way off this dance floor. But the music changed again and still she remained in his arms, swaying to the rhythm.

"Tell me," Beau said. "Didn't you girls have anything to say about the boys who could really dance?"

"I wouldn't know. I didn't make it to too many dances."

"Nobody good enough for you?" he teased.

She smiled at that improbable suggestion. There had been few dates for a skinny girl with glasses who was taller than half the boys in her class. Because she had had no desire to decorate the gymnasium wall, she hadn't left herself open to the humiliation of high-school dances.

It had been easier to stay at home, to tell herself that her mother needed her to help with Julie. In college there had been dates with young men who shared her serious attitude about grades. Then there had been Tom. Nowhere had there been time for dancing.

That she knew even the most basic of steps was due to her mother. Under Beverly's watchful eye, Caitlin had circled the living room with her equally skinny and awkward cousin Walter. She hoped Walter had had a moment like this, a few turns around a dance floor with a perfect partner.

Caitlin smiled up at Beau, forgetting that she had ever resisted dancing with him. If she never danced again, she could remember tonight. In his arms she felt like one of those girls who had never missed a school dance. He guided her through a series of spins, and she laughed, a breathless, excited laugh she scarcely recognized as her own.

"You should laugh more often," Beau told her.

"How do you know I don't laugh all the time?"

"You don't around me."

"That's because you're always making me angry."

He pretended to be serious. "I'm sorry. I'll try to be good from now on."

She giggled. "No, you won't."

"You're right."

Their laughter mingled. A comfortable sound, Caitlin thought.

"Quite seriously," Beau continued. "You need to laugh more."

"Not everyone leads a charmed, happy-go-lucky life like yours," she retorted.

"Oh, but that's the whole point. I have plenty of reasons to frown. I just choose to smile instead."

"I can't imagine what problems you could have." He was healthy, handsome and obviously successful. She doubted he could identify with one-tenth of the problems she had experienced.

His well-shaped lips pursed in a playful pout. "You'd be surprised what heartbreak is hidden by this smiling face."

"You, heartbroken? Now that really is something to laugh about," she replied, chuckling.

"Someday I'll tell you the whole tragic tale of my young life."

"That should make for light, entertaining fiction."

They laughed together again, and Beau's arms tightened around her. "See there. You don't *have* to walk around as if the sky were about to fall in."

"Maybe that's how I've felt ever since you came through my bathroom window."

"I'm sorry—"

"No, you're not. You enjoy turning people's lives upside down."

"Only if I think they need to be turned."

Caitlin's smile faded. Who was he to be judging a life he really knew very little about? The music ended, and she tried to move out of his arms.

"Don't start frowning now," he murmured. "You'll just make lines on that pretty face."

"It's not—"

"Yes it is a pretty face," he insisted. "I'm beginning to think you deny it just so you'll hear me say it again."

She gaped at him in astonishment. To try and elicit flattery from a man was completely alien to her. "You're ridiculous," she snapped. This time she succeeded in moving out of his embrace and through the crowd.

He caught her hand at the edge of the dance floor and turned her around to face him. Rather than cause a scene, Caitlin allowed him to lead her to an unoccupied spot at the railing that enclosed one side of the pavilion. Other couples had the same idea, but they were too engrossed in each other or the fast-darkening view of the ocean to pay any attention to two more people.

"I'd like to sit down now," Caitlin whispered as she pulled her hand from his.

Beau's voice was equally low and firm. "No, you wouldn't."

"Yes, I—"

"You'd rather dance."

"No—"

"Yes," he repeated. "You'd rather go back and dance every single dance. Because until you remembered to pull back into that shell of yours, you were having a good time."

"I..." Her denial faded as she faced the truth of his words. She had been enjoying herself. She did want to keep on dancing with him, despite how he irritated her.

His grin was impudent. "Admit it. You want to dance with me some more."

"Shouldn't..." She faltered, cleared her throat and continued, "Shouldn't you dance with Molly?"

"Why?" He leaned forward, bracing both hands on the railing, his arms on either side of her. His voice was husky. His lips a mere whisper away from hers. "Why should I dance with Molly when I'd rather dance with you?"

Caitlin's breath caught sharply. How was she supposed to think when his lips were so close? Those same lips had lingered on her skin only a little while ago. If she danced with him, he might kiss her again. And if he did... She swallowed. If Beau kissed her again...

While she hesitated, the music started again, and that was the deciding factor. With a man like Beau standing so close, Caitlin didn't know if there was a woman alive who could resist the gentle strains of "In the Still of the Night."

"Okay," she murmured. "Let's dance."

For a moment, just one heady moment, she thought he might kiss her then. But instead, in the smoothest of moves, he guided her back to the dance floor. There he twirled her around until she threw back her head and laughed, giddy with the feeling of freedom inside her. She didn't even mind his self-satisfied little grin.

The next morning Beau wondered when last night's dancing had stopped being a game. For at some point he had stopped worrying about teaching Caitlin to have fun and had begun to enjoy himself. They had danced entirely too long, forgetting that they had to be up bright and early for the first day of the shoot.

Funny thing was, he didn't feel at all tired as he helped Brenda and Pete carry equipment to the beach. He felt...well...the only words he could think of were *damned good*. Yes indeed, he felt damned good, better than he had felt in months. That feeling only got better when he saw Caitlin coming down the beach.

It was then that Beau realized he hadn't thought about anything *but* Caitlin for the last twelve or so hours. There'd been no late-night planning session with Molly. No nightmares about the agency. No urgent phone calls to the office this morning. And even realizing that she had occupied his thoughts more completely than any woman in the past four years didn't faze him. He still felt damned good.

He panicked for a moment. But only a moment. He had lost control for a little while last night, but he wouldn't again. Teaching Caitlin to loosen up was a game. Nothing more. She was just a woman. Nothing special. Feeling his usual confidence, he sent her his cockiest of smiles. Maybe today there'd be time for Lesson Number Two.

## *Chapter Four*

Caitlin sighed with satisfaction as she eased down into the king-size bathtub. After not taking a bubble bath since she was a kid, this was her second in only two days. For some reason she felt like indulging in every lazy, time-wasting impulse she'd ever had.

For some reason? Smiling, she sank lower in the tub. Beau was the reason. Beau and the unexpected attention he had been paying to her. He made her feel as if she deserved scented bath oils and strolls on the beach and the last dance of the evening. She was even beginning to believe him when he told her she was pretty.

Even when they were working, he was nice. Caitlin had expected him to be as bossy as he'd been during the session at Pete's studio. But he was merely firm. And always smiling. When he smiled it didn't seem to matter that she had been posing in the hot sun for hours. His smile smoothed away her nervousness, gave her confidence.

Perhaps her relaxed state of mind was part of the reason the shoot was going so well. They were well ahead of schedule. Yesterday they had moved from the beach to the pool to the tennis courts. Today, it had been the golf course and then inside to the restaurants. Tonight they were going to do some shots on the dance floor.

With Beau around it hardly seemed they were working. He kept everyone laughing. Yesterday he had organized an impromptu limbo contest during a break on the beach. Today he had given gaudy Hawaiian-print shirts to the whole group and insisted they wear them to lunch. How did he manage to be so completely off-the-wall and so disturbingly sexy at the same time?

And he was definitely sexy. Especially when he gave Caitlin his undivided attention, making her feel as if she were the only person on earth. She had told herself that feeling was ridiculous. Beau was simply being polite and friendly to her. Perhaps he felt a little guilty about practically railroading her into this job. He couldn't possibly be interested in her as anything more than an employee.

*Could he?*

The question was a good one, especially when the path Beau's lips had taken down Caitlin's neck still seemed to burn. Was that merely politeness? And was friendly the right description of the private after-midnight swim they had enjoyed last night? With her in her red swimsuit and him in his brief trunks, they might as well have been naked. At least it had felt that way when he had helped her out of the water. She had leaned against his hard, muscled body, lingering for perhaps a moment longer than necessary. The feel of him had been intoxicating, as magical as the carpet of stars above them and the flower-scented breeze. For a moment she had thought he would kiss her. She had wanted him to kiss her. She'd been wanting the same thing ever since.

Caitlin shivered, and realized her bathwater had cooled. She got out of the tub and dried off while giving herself a mental lecture. There was no use letting her foolish romantic notions get the best of her. Maybe Beau was flirting with her just a little. But flirting was second nature to him. She couldn't take it seriously. She should just relax and enjoy it.

A knock sounded at the door, and Brenda called, "Hurry up, Caitlin. I've got to do your hair and makeup. Pete wants you glamorous tonight."

Glamorous. Now that was a word Caitlin had never thought would be applied to herself. But then nothing that had happened to her in recent days was what she might have expected. Not the modeling. And certainly not Beau. Struggling to keep her mind off him, she hurried into underwear and a robe and went into the bedroom where Brenda was waiting.

As usual, she worked with quiet efficiency, transforming Caitlin into her glamorous alter ego. Her hair was brushed and fluffed and shaken, her lips were lined and colored and glossed, her lashes lengthened, her cheeks blushed, and her shoulders dusted with glittery powder. When Brenda was finished, Molly arrived with a freshly pressed dress for Caitlin to wear, a jade green confection of filmy, feminine gauze. She put it on, and turned back to the mirror.

Once again, Caitlin was amazed by what could be wrought by mascara and a curling iron and the right dress. Tonight, however, she didn't stand gaping at her transformed reflection. Tonight she stared at herself with wide, assessing eyes and said aloud the question that was most on her mind. "Do you think Beau will like how I look?"

Molly dropped a can of hair spray. Brenda was seized by a fit of coughing. Caitlin flushed and turned away from the mirror. She shouldn't have asked that. Now they would both know how silly she was. Sitting on the edge of the bed, she busied herself strapping on the sandals that matched her dress. The silence in the room was overpowering.

"I mean," she continued, striving to sound nonchalant, "Beau is so fussy about what I wear, and I was wondering if this was what he had in mind for tonight."

"Oh, I think he'll like it," Brenda murmured as she finished gathering tubes and powders and lipsticks into her makeup case. She grinned and winked at Caitlin before leaving the room.

Molly, however, was not smiling. She drew a chair close to the bed, her expression serious. "Caitlin, about Beau..." She paused and bit her lip. It was the look that prompted Beau to accuse her of being a mother hen.

Avoiding that concerned gaze, Caitlin stood. There was no use pretending she didn't know what Molly was trying to lead up to. Walking back to the mirror, she fussed with her hair. "I know what you're going to say."

"I just don't want you to be hurt."

"I don't think there's any chance of that." Caitlin turned around and heaved a sigh, leaning against the bureau. "I know I can't take anything he says or does seriously. To him I'm just a challenge." Hadn't he practically told her that on the first night they had danced?

Molly frowned. "You have to understand. Women have always been a game to Beau." She paused, regarding Caitlin with a thoughtful expression. "But he usually picks partners who are expert players."

Bristling, Caitlin started to protest.

"I don't mean any offense," Molly said quickly, standing. "But you wouldn't label yourself the playgirl type would you?"

"No, but—"

"Can you honestly say Beau is the kind of man you're usually interested in?"

"He's not, but—"

"But what?" Molly pressed.

"It's just that he's so...so..." Caitlin groped for the right words. "So attentive and nice, and he acts so interested in me."

"I'm not saying Beau isn't interested in you," Molly replied, looking as surprised by her words as Caitlin felt.

Hard put to keep the eagerness from her voice, she demanded, "Do you really think so?"

"Yes, I do." Molly appeared to regret her impulsive statement, and she rushed to add a note of caution. "But I still want you to be careful, Caitlin. Beau doesn't play for keeps."

"I could have guessed that."

"It's fun and games, and then it's over."

"I take it you've seen him through a few romances?"

"More than a few." Rather awkwardly, Molly patted Caitlin's arm. "Just don't get carried away, okay?"

"I won't."

The words were easy. The actions that went with them were a little tougher. Especially when Beau greeted Caitlin's appearance with an outrageous wolf whistle. Especially when he held her hand and gazed down into her eyes, giving her that we're-the-only-two-people-on-earth sensation. She wasn't going to ignore Molly's advice, but she also wasn't going to ignore the way he made her feel. For a woman who had never expected to find herself the object of such a man's attention, the sensation was exhilarating.

But it was just a game. And it would soon be over. Because sooner or later he would remember that her glamorous clothes and image were pure invention.

Caitlin paused on that thought. It was true she wasn't his type, but the woman she was pretending to be was. The woman who posed on the dance floor that evening with a handsome male model from Savannah was flirtatious, confident, sophisticated. That woman was Beau's own creation, and she could play his game—if only for a while.

*If* she really wanted to play.

With half a mind on what Pete was telling her to do, Caitlin looked around for Beau. She found him hovering nearby, on the fringe of the crowd that had gathered to watch them work. A week ago that crowd would have made her nervous. A week ago she would have distrusted the admiration in Beau's gaze. But a week ago she hadn't danced with him, hadn't felt his lips against her skin or swum with him under the stars. What a difference a week could make.

Did she want to play Beau's game? Caitlin found her answer in the smile he sent her way. What a persuasive smile that was. Only a fool would give up the chance for a taste of heaven, however small, however fleeting that taste might prove to be.

With that in mind she tossed her head and smiled back at him in what she hoped was a suitably provocative fashion. Pete, who was trying to get her attention, wasn't impressed. Beau, however, folded his arms across his chest and winked in that lazy, playful way of his. Caitlin felt rather pleased with herself.

Beau was feeling quite self-satisfied, too. His campaign to loosen Caitlin up was going well. Now she was relaxed and easy to work with. That was bound to show when these pictures were developed. The ads would be terrific. Richter would be pleased. And Beau, free of business worries, could ease up a little.

Already he'd felt more at peace during the last two days than he had in a long time. That was the other benefit of his Caitlin campaign. There was nothing like some sun, some sea, and the undivided attention of a woman to make a man forget his troubles. If he wasn't careful, he was going to forget everything, including the fact that his intentions toward her needed to remain strictly honorable. He rarely did more than flirt with employees, even temporary ones. The few exceptions he had made to that rule had turned into bona fide messes, and he couldn't afford any more difficulties than he already had.

But later that night, after dancing with Caitlin again, it was hard to resist the lure of a moonlit stroll on the beach. Especially when the stroll was her idea.

She was acting quite the little tease tonight, tossing her long hair, listening to his every word with wide-eyed wonder. She wasn't much like the former wallflower he had danced with only two nights ago. He knew an instant's regret at the change. He had enjoyed getting a rise out of her.

Leaving their shoes under a lifeguard's station, they set off down the darkened beach. Beau paused near the water's edge and rolled up his pant legs. The sand still held the heat of the sun, but the water was cool. Clouds had gathered, and the wind was sharper than usual, carrying the scent of rain. An occasional flash of lightning danced on the horizon, illuminating angry whitecaps far out at sea.

Caitlin hung back. "I'm always afraid I'll step on a jellyfish in the dark." Those stinging blobs of sea-life were all she remembered of her one childhood trip to the beach.

"Chicken," Beau teased. "We haven't seen a single jellyfish since we've been here."

"They've been waiting for us to venture out at night."

"Come on." Without ceremony he took hold of her hand and pulled her, still protesting, into the ankle-deep water. She gasped at the coldness, and he laughed. "As I keep saying, you have to live a little more dangerously. Where's the adventure in life if you don't take chances?"

Caitlin couldn't argue with that philosophy. Taking a chance was what had brought her to this beach in the first place. And that risk might be paying off. Her hand was still held in Beau's firm grasp. She took a further chance and threaded her fingers through his.

Her reward was a small, but nevertheless heart-stopping squeeze.

They strolled in companionable silence for several minutes before Beau spoke. "When I retire, I'm going to live on the ocean."

"Making retirement plans kind of early, aren't you?"

"I made these plans when I was ten." She laughed, but he continued in the same serious tone. "No joke. I've always planned to live by the ocean someday. When I was a kid, my parents used to rent a house for a month down on the Georgia coast. Dad never stayed the whole month—"

"Why not?"

Caitlin felt, rather than saw, the tightening of his expression. "My father was—and is—a very busy man," he explained in a voice so clipped it scarcely sounded as if it belonged to him. "A month was too long for him to be away from his law practice. But Mother and I always stayed. Loving the ocean is just about the only thing we ever had in common."

"My mother and I aren't much alike, either."

"It's different with me and my parents." There was the barest hint of anger in his tone now. "To my parents I'm just..." He stopped, as if considering how to explain himself.

He didn't continue, however, and although she was curious, Caitlin didn't push. There were enough skeletons in her own family closet to make her respectful of the privacy of others.

"You were telling me about your retirement plans," she prompted after they had walked for a few minutes in silence.

"I was?"

"The plans you made when you were ten."

"Oh, yeah." He chuckled, and Caitlin felt the tense muscles of his arm relax. "When my parents and I were at the beach, I wanted to stay outside day and night. Mother would put me to bed, and I'd sneak out the window and come down and look at the ocean."

Horrified, Caitlin imagined all the terrible fates that could befall a child alone in the dark on the beach.

"Bedtime was like every other rule my parents ever made—I broke them all."

"Now that doesn't surprise me," she said dryly.

"I suppose I was a holy terror. Mother, or Dad if he was there, would always check on me before going to bed, and sometimes I wouldn't make it back from the beach in time."

"I bet they were furious."

"That's a mild way of putting it," Beau said, his voice rueful. "I had plenty of other tricks, too. Like pouring sand in all the beds and leaving captured sea creatures in the sinks for Mother to find. Dad would always threaten to take me home if I didn't behave, and by the end of every vacation they would be swearing they'd never bring me back."

"But they always did, right?"

"Until I was ten. On our last night there, I sneaked out of the house and slept on the beach. Mother and Dad had called out the coast guard before anyone found me."

Having dealt with many mischievous children, Caitlin had plenty of sympathy for Beau's parents. "I think I would have killed you."

"I'm sure they thought about it. I know that at the time I would have preferred death to being grounded for a month when we got home."

"And they never brought you back to the beach?"

"Nope." The edge of anger was back in his voice. "Mother decided she'd rather vacation in the winter in the Bahamas. My summer vacation was an extra two weeks at camp. The next time I saw the ocean was spring break of my senior year in high school. I went down to Florida for a week and decided to stay for two."

"And you got in trouble again." Instead of a question, it was a simple statement of fact. She suspected Beau had stayed in trouble most of the time.

He laughed, and she imagined his eyes were twinkling in wicked delight. "I told you I was a holy terror."

"What was your punishment that time?"

He groaned. "The worst fate imaginable. A summer of hard labor at my father's office."

"That doesn't sound so bad."

He snorted. "You've obviously never spent much time in a law office. It isn't like they show it on television. There's lots of filing—endless filing—and all this talk about wherefors and thereupons and such nonsense."

"So you decided not to follow in your father's footsteps?"

"Oh, I had already decided against that. In the fall I headed for Knoxville and played football and chased coeds and majored in advertising."

"What did your parents think about that?"

"They wanted me to go to Harvard." Beau pretended to shiver. "God, I can't imagine spending four years with those frigid northern women."

"You're terrible," Caitlin declared, giggling. "Plenty of people would die for the chance at an Ivy League education."

"You included?"

"Me included."

"Where did you go to college?"

"Same as you, the University of Tennessee," Caitlin answered, not without pride. Scholarships and part-time jobs had paid her way through college.

"So we're both alumni of one of the country's true party schools."

She shook her head. "You and I attended two different colleges, Mr. Collins. I spent my time studying—not at beer busts, or frat parties or football games." She knew the type of student Beau had probably been, the kind who borrowed notes from missed classes and only darkened the library door the night before a big test.

"I'll have you know that I studied and graduated cum laude," he said defensively. "Without grades the old man wouldn't foot the bill for college—any college."

"Couldn't you have gotten a football scholarship?"

"That wouldn't have been fair to someone who really needed the help."

The selflessness of that reply wasn't in keeping with the portrait of a privileged rebel he had been painting for Caitlin. But it told her more than all the tales of childhood pranks and college capers. And it made her like him all the more. "You really are kind of a nice guy, aren't you?"

"Me? Nice?" Pretending to be insulted, he dropped her hand, bent over and splashed water up the front of her dress. "I've never been nice in my whole life." He splashed her again and still again, until she ran away, shrieking.

They chased each other like children through the shallow waves, drenching each other's clothes, not stopping until Beau swept Caitlin up in his arms and carried her farther into the surf. He intended to drop her in, but his plans changed. Quickly. For there was nothing childish about the feelings aroused by the brush of his hand across the soaked bodice of her dress, nothing childlike in the sudden stilling of her struggles. That was all it took for the mood to change completely. And that was when he kissed her.

Caitlin had been waiting for this moment. This kiss was the whole reason she had flirted with him and invited him to walk on the beach. She had wanted to play Beau's game. She should have been prepared. But when is anyone ever prepared for a thunderbolt?

He kissed as he lived. Boldly. No patient sweetness for Beau. He went straight to the heart of the matter, taking every inch of her mouth with reckless, relentless daring. And when her senses were reeling, he changed tactics, his lips turning gentle and coaxing. Like a tennis player who opens a game with a smashing serve, he now seemed content with long, apparently effortless volleys.

His arms loosened, and her body began a slow slide down the long, hard length of his. Soon they were both standing in water that swirled to her knees, and still he kissed her. Or was she kissing him? She couldn't imagine that it mattered. The important thing was that they go on kissing. Forever, if possible.

The spur-of-the-moment kiss had turned into something much more serious for Beau. Lost in her sweet woman's scent, he let his fingers tangle in her damp hair. She moaned softly against his mouth, and his body hardened. His hand slid down her back and settled on her curving bottom, and he pulled her hips hard against his own. God, what a feeling. What aching, perfect torture. Any doubts about Caitlin's untapped passions were banished forever as she continued to respond to his kiss. He'd been right. Those passions were just waiting to be explored by the right man.

The ocean brought his thoughts and his body under control, choosing that moment to slap them with a wave of unusual force. Pulling back from Caitlin, Beau noticed that the wind had picked up and the smell of rain was sharper than ever.

"Come on," he yelled, tugging her toward the shore. "It's going to pour."

Caitlin couldn't imagine why that mattered, since they were already soaking wet, but she didn't argue. It took all of her concentration just to move, and if it hadn't been for Beau, she probably would have collapsed into the sand. Talking was impossible. The waves crashed and the wind screamed and her own heart was beating so loud it echoed inside her head. *He had kissed her.*

With trembling fingers she touched her mouth, imagining that it was still warm from the pressure of his. Logic told her not to be preposterous. Emotion encouraged her to hang on to this gossamer sensation of desire.

There was, however, no time for reflection. Chased by the elements, they retrieved their shoes and made it to the dance pavilion just before the storm hit. The lights had been dimmed, the restaurant side of the building closed off against the wind and rain. A few brave souls had stayed behind to watch the storm. More sound than substance, it blew itself out in only a few minutes and made Caitlin wish she and Beau had remained on the beach.

Damn the storm, anyway, she thought. Without the interruption, that spectacular kiss might have been followed by something more than this awkward, growing silence. In the dim light it was impossible to read Beau's expression, but he wasn't smiling. That was a bad sign, considering this was a man who could smile even when faced with a loaded gun.

Nervous, she ran a hand through her damp hair and brushed at her wet dress. "I guess I should...uh...go back to the condo...or something."

Beau could only nod and wish she would leave her dress alone. Were the gestures unconscious or did she know how sexy she looked? There was just enough light for him to see the way her dress pulled against her small but rounded breasts. And the material was just thin enough to emphasize the pert thrust of her nipples. She shivered, the tips of her breasts grew even more distinct, and it was with an effort that he brought his gaze back up to her face. But what he found in her expression was even more disturbing.

The glamorous makeup she had worn for the evening's work had been washed away by the wind and rain and ocean water. Faint smudges, like bruises, colored the delicate skin beneath her eyes. And what eyes they were. Wide. Darker than usual. Vulnerable-looking. The guilt that had been building ever since that moment on the beach closed around Beau's gut and squeezed. He had put that look in her eyes.

"Let's go," he muttered and took hold of her elbow. She needed to be tucked safely into bed, well away from him.

Neither of them said a word as they hurried through the resort's grounds. The clubhouse was still brightly lit, with music and laughter spilling from the opened windows, and Beau figured the rest of their group could be found inside. Sure enough, when they reached the condominium it was dark and deserted. The last thing he needed right now was to be alone with Caitlin. Smothering a curse, he flipped on the lights in the living area and headed back for the door. "I'm going over to the clubhouse," he said, not looking at where she stood at the bottom of the stairs. "You get out of those wet things and make an early night of it, why don't you?" His hand closed on the doorknob.

"Beau?"

He shut his eyes, not wanting to respond to her soft query. Maybe if he just opened the door and walked—

"Beau?"

There was no quick escape. He had to face her again. Somehow he managed to smile and turn around. She was regarding him with those big, too-innocent eyes.

"Are you going to leave like that?"

Like what, he wondered, panicking. What was Caitlin expecting?

"I mean," she explained, "don't you want your shoes?"

His gaze dropped to the loafers that dangled from her hands. Only then did he realize that he was still barefoot and that the shoes clutched in his left hand were hers. In their haste to get out of the rain, they had each grabbed the other's shoes.

The faintest trace of a grin played about her lips. "I think you'd look pretty silly in my sandals."

Beau held up the slim, strappy shoes. "You think so?"

"They'd clash with your pants."

"I could change."

She giggled, and the strained atmosphere between them relaxed. Grinning sheepishly, Beau tossed her sandals on the stairs, took his loafers and slipped them on. "I should probably change anyway," he said, glancing at his wet, wrinkled slacks. "No telling what they'll think I've been doing if I show up at the clubhouse looking like this."

"Yes, no telling," Caitlin echoed softly. "Although you... we... haven't done anything..." The *yet* that belonged at the end of that sentence dangled enticingly between them, unspoken but clearly implied.

Beau's glance skittered back to her face. Dammit, there she went again, looking all soft and sweet and inviting. And if she were any other woman, he might just take her up on that invitation. Hell, he thought as he took a step toward her, maybe he'd take her up on it anyway.

His sanity returned with the caution that crept into her eyes. That caution was what set her apart. Women who knew the rules weren't cautious at all, probably because they had nothing to lose. Well, Caitlin certainly didn't know the rules. Until a few days ago, she'd been hiding behind her glasses and her unattractive clothes and her serious attitude. And maybe she was better off hidden, Beau thought. She was too fragile, too easily broken to even be thinking of playing his kind of game. He could hurt her if he wasn't careful, and being careful had never been one of his strong points.

Besides her feelings, there was Richter's account to think about. Getting involved with Caitlin could only complicate this project, and he didn't need that. She needed to stay loose and relaxed. But if she kept looking at him with those big hazel eyes, things were going to get very tight and tense. He had to leave before his natural inclinations overrode his good intentions.

He stepped backward. "I think I will run over to the clubhouse."

"But your clothes—"

"They'll dry." Without glancing back, he crossed to the door and left.

Caitlin sank down on the stairs. She wasn't sure if her legs were trembling from relief or disappointment. What had possessed her to try to get him to stay? What would she have done if he had? The romantic possibilities popped along her nerves with such force that the room seemed to spin around her. She took a deep breath.

*Tomorrow.* Yes, there was tomorrow. Tomorrow she would act as if nothing had happened. That was obviously what Beau wanted. Tonight she would sit here for a little while and relive that kiss and the steamy look that had been in his eyes before he had left for the clubhouse. But tomorrow she would forget it. Tomorrow she would be cool, calm and collected. At least she hoped so, Caitlin added, beginning to panic.

* * *

Early evening shadows were spreading across the lawn when Beau drew his rental car to a halt in his parents' driveway. He paused for a moment, wondering why he had come. Then, resolutely, he got out of the car and headed down the flower-edged walk to the three-story brick-and-stone home. "Damn Melissa, anyway," he grumbled as he mounted the front steps.

For it was his cousin Melissa who was responsible for Beau's presence at his parents' home in Chattanooga. Strictly speaking, that wasn't the whole truth. His being in the city at all was due to a frantic phone call he had received from his office late last night. Beau could have sent Molly to handle the crisis, but the emergency had provided him with a convenient excuse to get away from Caitlin for a while. He knew Caitlin would be surprised, perhaps even hurt by his sudden disappearance. But he also knew it was for her own good.

"So this is Caitlin's fault," he muttered, punching the doorbell. If Caitlin hadn't rattled him so badly, he wouldn't have come to Chattanooga, and he wouldn't have had lunch with Melissa. Then Melissa couldn't have told him how bad his father looked, and Beau wouldn't have fallen prey to an attack of guilt. Without the guilt he wouldn't have called his father, and he wouldn't have accepted an invitation to dinner. Although Beau still might not have felt guilty if it hadn't been three months since he had seen either of his parents.

"So I guess this is really *my* fault." After admitting that, he pressed the bell again, just as his mother swung the door open.

"Beau, dear, there's no need to keep on and on with the bell," Martha Collins admonished in her clear, crisp voice. "And what's your fault?"

Beau had to smile. How like his mother to skip the pleasantries. "Everything's my fault," he said, bending to brush the obligatory kiss across her cheek. "Everything's always my fault."

"Please don't talk nonsense." She gestured for him to come inside and closed the door. Only then did her blue eyes soften. "It is good to see you, Son. We've missed you."

For his undemonstrative mother, those were highly emotional words, and they surprised Beau. He wanted to believe she meant them. He had missed her. Even considering the gulf that had grown between them, she was still his mother, and he loved her. He slipped an arm around her shoulders as they headed across the foyer. "You look beautiful," he said.

"Thank you." She inclined her head, as if the words were nothing more than her just due. Then she astonished Beau by smoothing a hand down her hips and adding, "I've put on weight since the last time you were here."

He reassured her with a negative shake of his head. If she was heavier than the last time they'd been together, then the pounds sat well on her slender figure. Her hair, still more blond than gray, was cut in a new, more youthful style, and there didn't seem to be many more lines in the delicate skin around her eyes and mouth. Age, like the pearls that rimmed her slender throat, only enhanced Martha Collins's beauty.

"Your father is late," she said, leading Beau into the family room.

"Am I supposed to be surprised?"

"Now, Beau."

Ignoring her soft rebuke, he settled into a comfortable arm chair. The room, like his mother, hadn't really changed in years. Done in warm browns and yellows, it was the homiest spot in the large, decorator-perfect house. "I'm glad you haven't changed anything in here," Beau told his mother. "This was always my favorite room."

"Your father's, too."

Considering how little time his father had spent in this room, Beau could have made a sarcastic retort, but he thought better of it. No matter what he said, his mother would always take up for his father. Why waste time arguing?

She sat down on the couch and gave him a small smile. "I had the cook make all your favorites for dinner, and I baked a chocolate cake."

"*You* baked a cake?"

"Don't look so amazed," Martha retorted, touching her pearls in a nervous gesture. "I used to make you chocolate cakes all the time when you were a boy."

"It's just been a while since I was a boy, Mother."

The look she gave him was long and searching and somewhat sad. Or so it seemed to Beau. But perhaps he was mistaken, for the sadness was replaced by a bright smile as she stood up and headed for the small bar in the corner of the room. "I guess what I really should be making you is a drink. The usual whiskey and water, like your father, right?"

Beau nodded and watched her for a moment, following each of her smooth, economical movements. Her gracefulness reminded him of Caitlin. Even when she was feeling insecure and trying to look plain,

Caitlin had exuded the same unconscious poise that set his mother apart. Strange that two such disparate women should share that quality. His mother's life had always been filled with everything that was beautiful and refined. Her family was wealthy. Her husband was a man of influence and power in the community. Her brother—Melissa's father—was an ex-congressman. While Caitlin...

Pausing, Beau realized he knew very little about Caitlin's life or background. She was a teacher, she had a very charming mother, and she lived in Hunt's apartment building. That was basically all he knew, unless he could count the knowledge that she turned to liquid fire when kissed in just the right way.

That last thought made him grin, and he was so lost in remembering Caitlin's kiss that it took him a moment to realize his mother was handing him a drink.

She raised one smooth eyebrow. "At least whatever has you so absorbed appears to be pleasant."

Instead of answering, Beau sipped his drink. It bothered him that he had been preoccupied by thoughts of Caitlin. That had happened over and over again today. He had to get her out of his mind.

"Is she anyone your father and I know?" his mother continued, a sly look in her eye.

Beau laughed. "What you really want to know is whether she's someone I've brought up to meet you before."

"Nonsense." The reply came just a shade too quickly.

"Just rest easy, Mother. She's no one you know," Beau retorted, thinking of the parade of unsuitable women he had brought to his mother's table. Caitlin wasn't like any of them, not even remotely so. She also wasn't likely to wind up at his parents' table. Or if she did, it wouldn't be as one of his women. Realizing he was dwelling on Caitlin again, he quickly changed the subject. "Mother, Melissa told me Father isn't looking well. How is he feeling?"

"Fit as a fiddle." The booming reply came from the doorway, and both Beau and his mother got up as Beauregard Perris Collins III—Perry to friends and family—came into the room.

"Please, both of you, sit down," Perry added, coming forward. But instead of sitting, Martha hurried to make him a drink while Beau shook his father's hand.

As usual he felt as if he should be saluting. His father was no taller than he, but there was something very stiff and military in his bearing. His once-red hair was mostly white, his angular face was lined, but his shoulders were still as straight and broad as ever, his green eyes snapping with life. He was a man who had always commanded respect from everyone, including his son.

Perry settled on the couch with his drink and regarded Beau with suspicion. "So now I know why you called today."

"Sir?"

"Melissa's been spreading rumors about my health."

"She was concerned," Beau admitted.

"As you can see, the rumors are unfounded."

"They appear to be."

"You can settle Melissa's fears," Perry added, something akin to amusement lightening his stern countenance. "But I'm glad to see you, even if you are only checking me out."

"Perry," Martha admonished.

He chuckled. "Just checking to see if you might be coming into your inheritance early, isn't that right, Son?"

Despite the laughter, Beau went immediately on guard. Was his father saying he knew his son needed money? Perhaps, as he'd feared, his father had heard about his financial troubles and was waiting for a chance to gloat.

Tense now, Beau couldn't recapture the almost lighthearted atmosphere he had maintained with his mother. They finished their drinks. They had dinner. His father kept up a running commentary on a wide assortment of safe topics—baseball, politics, his mother's chocolate cake. But for Beau the evening grew increasingly strained. He kept waiting for Perry to make another jab, to criticize him in some way.

Remarkably, however, they made it through the meal without anything being said about Beau's shortcomings. He imagined that was a lifetime record. Not wishing to push his luck, he made his excuses soon afterward. Although it could have been his imagination, his mother's goodbye hug seemed genuine. But the real surprise was when his father walked him out to his car.

The man didn't say much. He puffed on his pipe, mostly, and made Beau wonder why he hadn't just said goodbye in the house. Finally, when Beau opened his car door, Perry spoke, his voice gruff. "I...uh...I hope you won't stay away so long this time. Your mother worries about you."

That was news to Beau, but he didn't argue.

His father continued, "I'd like..." He paused and cleared his throat. "I'd like to see more of you myself."

"Yes, sir," Beau murmured obediently, even as he wondered what his father was up to. The man obviously wanted something. He could be very nice when he wanted his son to conform to some standard he thought appropriate.

But Perry asked for nothing. He awkwardly patted his son on the shoulder and turned to go. "Just stay in touch, and let me know if there's anything I can do for you." He started back down the driveway before Beau could reply.

He wouldn't have replied even if his father had stayed. For the man's innocent-sounding words had touched off a white-hot fury inside Beau. Since when was his father willing to do anything for him?

Oh, he had provided a home and an education and every material thing anyone could want. But he had never been a father, at least not in the sense that Beau had wanted him to be. He had never listened. He had never considered what Beau might want. He had been too worried about his precious law firm and the precious family name to consider that his son was an individual. Beau was an heir, not a son. Having assured the continuance of the Collins name, his father had considered his duty done.

That attitude might have worked if Beau had been a different sort of person, if he had been docile and obedient and somewhat less of a rebel. But he was what he was, and that had always been a disappointment to his parents.

He slammed into his car and gunned the motor, imagining that his father was wincing at the sound.

Then he tore off down the drive, knowing that his parents hated it when he drove that way. Almost immediately, he felt guilty and eased up on the accelerator. He wasn't seventeen anymore. He couldn't hope to get his parents' attention by breaking their rules.

Why was it still so important to prove something to them? he wondered. He wasn't like them. He could never be like them. Bound by traditions, they spent their days keeping up appearances. They lived in the Collins's family home on Lookout Mountain alongside Chattanooga's other wealthy and privileged citizens. His mother volunteered for the right charities and wore the right clothes. His father made the right investments and supported the right political candidates. They were a credit to the Collins name. They rarely took risks or raised their voices or made mistakes. So how the hell had they ended up with a son like Beau?

The question was an old one and had no answer. But Beau continued to ask it as he took the winding road down the mountain and into the heart of Chattanooga. No, he could never be what his parents had hoped for. But somehow, some way they were going to approve of him. Someday soon they would be congratulating him on his business success. And maybe then he would bring the "right" sort of woman to their house for dinner. Maybe someone like Caitlin.

Remembering Caitlin, the last of his anger eased out of Beau. Yes, his mother would approve of her, even if she didn't have ancestors who were among the founding fathers of the state. She could put up her hair and wear something demure and correct, and his mother would smile and beam approvingly. And Beau would sit across the table and imagine that Caitlin was

"Clothes," Caitlin echoed, getting up and opening the closet door. "Clothes are a problem. I've got the things we bought for the shoot, but I can't wear them all the time, and I'm already sick of just about everything else I brought with me."

"I smell a shopping spree," Brenda announced, bouncing off the bed and to her feet. "We've got hours before we have to be packed and out of here. Let's catch the hotel's shuttle bus over to the mall and hit the shops."

Caitlin soon discovered that shopping sprees were serious business when Brenda was involved. They launched what could only be called an attack on the June sales and quickly disposed of a big chunk of Caitlin's modeling fee. But for the first time in her life, she didn't think money spent on clothes was a waste. It helped that Brenda's eye for a bargain was as sharp as her sense of style.

"The price is right, and the color is definitely you," she said as Caitlin turned around in front of a dressing-room mirror. The clingy knit sundress she had slipped on was fuchsia, and its short, flounced skirt revealed plenty of tanned thigh.

"Isn't it a little daring?"

"Beau likes daring women."

Caitlin was still doubtful, but Brenda was insistent. "Trust me," she said. "He'll love it." She directed a worried look at her watch. "However, he will not love us if we don't hurry. We're supposed to leave for Savannah in less than an hour, and we've still got to pack." She unpinned the tags from Caitlin's dress. "We'll pay for this and tell the salesclerk you'll just wear it home."

"You're almost as bossy as my mother," Caitlin grumbled, stuffing the clothes she'd worn to the mall into a bag.

"I'm sure she's a charming woman." The smile Brenda directed over her shoulder was full of mischief, but her voice assumed all the sweetness of a drill sergeant's. "Come on, shake the lead out!"

They hurried back to the resort to find Molly pacing the floor and trying to pack everyone's suitcases. They were in such a rush that it wasn't until Caitlin stood in the lobby of the hotel, waiting for one of the resort's vans that she had time to think about Beau. And immediately she wished she hadn't. Thinking about Beau was like putting her insides through a food processor. She'd stay healthier if he stayed out of her thoughts.

She fiddled nervously with the gold bangle bracelets Brenda had insisted she buy. They weren't the sort of jewelry she would have chosen for herself, but she supposed they matched her dress. She glanced down, noticing again how short her skirt was. The dress wasn't exactly her, either. Or was it? That depended on who she was pretending to be—her true self or the glamorous woman who posed in front of Pete's camera.

Pretense was the operative word. The more she pretended to be that other woman, the blurrier the lines between illusion and reality became. Perhaps the smartest move would be to reserve her playacting for the camera. But Beau wouldn't be interested in plain old Caitlin. It was the other woman, the made-up, dressed-up doll that he had kissed. Wasn't it?

*Here I go again,* Caitlin thought, *obsessing about him. When did that man become so important to me?*

Knowing she had to stop thinking about him or drive herself crazy, she glanced around the lobby. Her gaze collided with that of a man waiting in line at the registration desk. Boldly, he looked her up and down, and there was no mistaking the appreciation in his expression. Flattered but uncomfortable with his perusal, Caitlin was glad when the van pulled to a stop outside the lobby's glass doors.

Their luggage was loaded, and she stepped into the van, only to meet another set of admiring male eyes. The driver was young, probably a college student working a summer job, and there was nothing subtle in the whistle he directed her way. "Yes, ma'am," he said. "This is one trip to Savannah that will be a pleasure."

Everyone laughed, and Brenda sent her an I-told-you-so look.

But rather than be forced into a conversation with the driver, Caitlin took a seat in the back of the van. She was quiet as they pulled away from the resort. She wasn't used to all this attention from men, and she wasn't entirely sure that she liked it. Maybe that was silly of her. Maybe other women wanted to be admired from afar. But the admiration of one special person seemed infinitely more appealing than the appreciation of any number of strangers.

Caitlin knew that if things had worked out differently, she would have been content with the love and admiration of Tom Leland. Tom certainly hadn't fallen for her on the basis of her looks. Oh, he had often complimented her. But his were a lover's compliments, an admittedly prejudiced view, and she hadn't taken them seriously. Her relationship with him had been on a slightly more cerebral level. Perhaps too cerebral she thought, frowning. Never had he reduced her to the quivering mass of want just one glance from Beau Collins could produce.

And this chemistry working between her and Beau wasn't entirely physical, either. Though certainly no sophisticate, Caitlin could recognize and handle mere sexual attraction. But it was Beau—the complete man—who fascinated her, and there was more to the complete man than met the eye. More than the handsome face and hard, thoroughly male body. More than the quick laughter and ready smile. Beneath the exterior flash was the real man she had only glimpsed so far.

That man was passionate about his business. Maybe too passionate, she decided, remembering the zeal with which he had pursued her for this project. He was a man who had been hurt by his family. For only hurt could produce the bitterness in his voice when he had spoken of his parents. And though he probably didn't realize it and wouldn't admit it, he was a sensitive person. A less perceptive man would have taken Caitlin up on the rather blatant invitation she had issued two nights before. But he had known it wasn't right for her. He had walked away. And that action had captivated her more than a night of passion ever could.

Although nights—and mornings and afternoons—of passion might not be such a bad thing, she thought. Before her mind could go any further in that direction, their driver announced that they were coming into Savannah.

The bridge they crossed was a magnificent span of steel and concrete, and Caitlin thought it a very modern gateway to a city firmly rooted in the past. Born on the banks of the Savannah River, the city was the oldest in Georgia. Restoration efforts in recent years had carefully preserved the ambiance of a bygone era.

At Molly's urging their driver took them along historic Bay and River Streets. Here, he explained, cotton exporters known as factors had once plied their trade in the multistoried warehouses that faced the riverfront. These warehouses were now homes to restaurants, shops and galleries, making the stone-paved River Street a center of commerce and activity.

The rest of Savannah's historic district appeared to be just as carefully preserved, a picture of elegance cut from the fabric of the past. Giant, moss-covered oaks shaded gracious homes and flower-bedecked squares. Groups of tourists were sightseeing on foot or from the picturesque comfort of horse-drawn carriages. Behind one such vehicle, the van drew to a halt.

Caitlin could easily see that this Plantation House hotel was completely different from the resort they had left barely an hour before. Molly explained that the building had been used as an inn since the 1800s, and when Richter had purchased it, he had also obtained the house behind. Both buildings had been modernized without sacrificing any of their original charm, and the result was a spacious inn of some elegance.

"This is more like it," Caitlin commented as they climbed out of the van. "I can really imagine Scarlett O'Hara visiting here."

"Then it should be easy to get into character."

At the sound of Beau's voice, she whirled around. Now why did the sight of him make the two days they had been apart seem like an eternity?

He didn't give her a chance to say anything. Instead his gaze swept down her, and his grin was slow and teasing. Infinitely sexy. The heat that built inside her had nothing to do with the ninety-five-degree temperature. "I like your outfit, Scarlett," he teased in that drawling way of his. "It looks..." He paused, and glanced down at her bare legs. "It looks very cool."

"It is." Caitlin discovered it was hard to talk when one felt more like gasping for a breath. Her imagination might be getting the best of her, but it seemed as if his eyes held a promise. A hot, male, infinitely delicious promise.

"Hey, Beau," Pete called, interrupting their perusal of each other. "Are you going to stand there or help me carry some of this equipment inside?"

Beau was tempted to tell Pete to get a bellboy to help him, but he knew that not just anyone was allowed to touch the man's cameras and lights. "I'm coming," he said with reluctance, and he turned to admire Caitlin's legs as she climbed the steps to the inn's entrance.

Pete's smile was knowing. "Our moth is changing into a butterfly."

"Maybe." Beau bent to pick up a camera case. Pete merely chuckled.

But later Beau decided Pete was right. Caitlin was a moth, and so was he. And both of them were flying too close to a flame he couldn't quite label.

It wasn't anything either of them said. They barely spoke to each other. Between them, however, an awareness simmered. The tension was there in every exchange of glances during dinner. It didn't help that their meal was served in the cool, romantic beauty of the small walled garden that adjoined the inn's restaurant. Bordered by wisteria and fragrant with jasmine, the garden featured a small fountain where water splashed in a musical cadence.

Beau found himself wishing that everyone but Caitlin would just fade away. He would have liked to sit in this sweet-smelling garden with her, sipping a mint julep and watching the evening shadows deepen into night. Later, they could stroll down the oak-lined street, and perhaps in the shadow of some century-old house he would kiss her again.

But that scenario was only a wish, a distracting, farfetched notion. For he and Caitlin were not alone, and there was no time for twilight strolls. There was work to be done.

After dinner Caitlin changed into antebellum attire for two of the shots that would form the backgrounds for the ads. In one she stood at the bottom of a curving stairway, fan raised to her chin, gazing over her shoulder. In the other she lounged on an antique settee, wide skirts spread over the brocade upholstery, eyes suitably dreamy.

The shots were a nightmare of lighting and shadow and positioning, a task made more difficult by the hotel guests who kept interrupting. Even worse were the distracted states of Beau and Caitlin. When Pete would consult Beau about a shot, the question often had to be repeated. Caitlin was just as slow to react to instructions. But when they looked at each other—oh, now that was a different story—then their concentration could barely be broken.

Everyone was short-tempered and exhausted by the time they were finished, but instead of going to his room Beau retreated to one of the inn's many fragrant, dimly-lit gardens. He sipped bourbon instead of a mint julep, and he wished Caitlin was seated across from him. Her eyes had been full of invitation tonight. Was she serious? More important, could he resist her for much longer?

If he followed his instincts and became involved with her, he would be breaking his own rules. He might even jeopardize this project and therefore the whole account and his business. But he wondered if the risks might be worth the prize. For Caitlin was a prize. Of that he was sure. Weren't all the best presents found in the most tightly wrapped packages?

Taken by the notion of undoing the last of Caitlin's well-tied bows, Beau grinned and raised his glass in a silent salute.

"Okay, gang, I think that's all for today," Pete announced, dropping onto a bench in one of the inn's courtyards. "It's just too damned hot to work any more."

Nodding her grateful agreement, Caitlin sank wearily to the bench opposite his. Brenda and Molly didn't even bother with seats, electing instead to sprawl on a shady patch of grass beneath a tree.

Caitlin thought they should have knocked off hours ago, but with tomorrow's weather forecast calling for rain, they had tried to complete all the outdoor shots today. Their efforts had been hampered by groups of curious onlookers who had constantly walked through Pete's carefully staged attempts to capture the charm of the inn's historic surroundings.

Adding to the frustration was the heat. Natives had assured the group that a temperature reading in the high nineties wasn't at all unusual for late June, but Caitlin wondered how anything was ever accomplished in the humid, oppressive air. It had completely sapped her energy. Of course, she admitted silently, a good night's rest would have probably helped. She should have gone to bed instead of sitting in her room's window seat, staring down at the garden where Beau had stayed until the early hours of the morning.

Thinking of Beau she glanced around, half expecting to see him striding down one of the flower-edged paths. He had disappeared into the inn more than an hour before, soon after they had set up his last shot. While the rest of them had been grumbling and complaining about the heat, he had been almost unbearably cheerful all day. His lack of sleep didn't appear to have troubled him in the least.

What had kept him awake? In the cover of darkness with only Molly's sleep-evened breathing for company, Caitlin had dared to imagine that Beau might be thinking of her. That possibility had almost literally tied her in knots. Arms clasped to her chest and feet tucked beneath her, she had huddled on her seat and relived every glance they had exchanged since that afternoon. He had watched her all night long. Speculative, inviting and admiring, the look in his eyes had disarmed her completely. She wondered if he could follow every sensual turn her thoughts had taken.

The cheerful sound of whistling roused Caitlin from her musing. Without turning to look, she knew it was Beau. Who else could sound so completely carefree at the end of such a long, tiring day?

"What's wrong with you guys?" he demanded, sprawling on the bench beside Caitlin. Quickly, she looked away from the length of muscled thigh revealed by his navy-blue shorts. Not that the tanned expanse of skin made any difference. She was always intensely aware that he was a man, no matter what he wore.

The others filled him in on their aching feet, sunburned noses and throbbing headaches.

Beau didn't seem impressed. "So none of you could be tempted into a dinner down on River Street?"

Molly's answer was emphatic. "I'm going to soak these feet, call my man and make it an early night."

"And Pete and I are planning an evening alone," Brenda supplied with an impish grin.

Her husband groaned. "Which means I had better go up and get some rest now."

While everyone laughed, Beau turned to Caitlin. "I guess that leaves you and me. Are you too exhausted for a walk down to the river for some seafood?"

Ten minutes earlier she'd been wondering where she would find the energy to make it to her room. But the thought of dinner—alone—with Beau rejuvenated her. Ignoring the look that passed between Molly and Brenda, she nodded and tipped her head back so that her glance met his. "I'd love some good seafood."

"Great," he murmured, his smile pleased. "I'll meet you down here about seven, all right?" She nodded again, wondering why even his most casual smile could bring all her senses sharply to life.

Beau ambled to his feet. "Come on, Pete. I'll help you carry that tripod. It sounds as if you need to conserve your strength for tonight."

The men, trailed by Brenda, headed inside. Molly remained on the grass. Caitlin stayed on the bench, half expecting another lecture from her companion. But Molly surprised her.

"You should wear that new white dress you and Brenda bought," she advised, getting up.

"I should?"

"Yes, and you can borrow my best perfume and my favorite earrings. Beau'll never know what hit him."

Caitlin didn't move, gaping at Molly in amazed stupefaction. When had the woman changed her mind about Caitlin becoming involved with Beau?

"Are you just going to sit there?" Molly asked, bending to retrieve her ever-present clipboard. "Get up, and let's go make you beautiful." Grinning, Caitlin complied.

Later, as she walked through the courtyard, she felt Molly's efforts had been successful. Especially when Beau turned from his study of the nearby street and let his gaze slip over her. That gaze lingered like a caress on skin left nearly bare by her dress's off-the-shoulder neckline. He didn't say a word, but he didn't have to. She could read the approval in his eyes.

Silently, she approved of him, too. In cotton slacks and a white polo shirt he looked both cool and casual, making her glad she had foregone hose and heels in favor of sandals.

"It's still really hot," he said, taking her hand in what seemed the most natural of gestures. "Are you sure you want to walk?"

"It's not so bad compared with this afternoon. At least there's a breeze."

"And so what if that breeze feels as if it were blowing straight from an oven, right?"

She smiled. "Right." Hot or not, the slight stirring of air felt good against her skin as they strolled toward the river.

Beau was silent, content to listen to Caitlin's commentary on the sights they passed. She had a way of sounding so utterly fascinated with the world around her that he couldn't help but be fascinated, too. In truth it was Caitlin more than their surroundings that captured his interest. She was that rare woman who wasn't constantly demanding to be entertained. Although perhaps that quality wasn't such a rarity, he amended. Perhaps he had just been hanging out with the wrong women. It bothered him—for one fleeting moment—that his thought was just like something his parents might have said.

Whatever the case, he found it incredibly restful to walk beside this pretty woman in her pretty white cotton dress. With her, there was pleasure in even the simplest of actions—pausing to admire a colorful cascade of flowers or listening to her laughter or keeping a tight hold on her hand as they hurried across a busy intersection. It was easy to be with her. In that simplicity Beau knew there was also a danger. For he knew it would take very little to ease into an involvement with Caitlin. Strangely enough that danger didn't make him back off. Instead, anticipation stirred inside him.

The seafood restaurant that had been recommended to Beau was housed in one of the old cotton warehouses that lined River Street. It was easy to find, but dinner was delayed because Caitlin had to stop and admire every building they passed. "I'm surprised we made it here at all," Beau teased after they had placed their order. "Are you sure you don't want to inspect every cobblestone in the street out front?"

She looked embarrassed. "I'm sorry if I was boring you. I'm sort of a history buff, and this area is so well preserved that I—"

"It's okay. History was never my favorite subject, but you manage to make it all sound very interesting. I can see that you're a good teacher."

The waiter interrupted by bringing the bottle of wine Beau had ordered. "Very nice," Caitlin said approvingly after taking a sip.

"Are you a wine connoisseur?"

She blinked. "Aren't you?" He had taken such care in ordering from the wine list that she had assumed he was an expert.

His grin was impudent. "Of course not. All I know about wine is that it comes in different colors. But I always look over the wine list to impress the waiter. If you'll notice, I took his suggestion. I bet we get great service all through the meal."

"That's very sneaky."

"But it works."

"And what happens when you're in the company of someone who truly is an expert?" Caitlin asked, amused.

"I wing it."

"Well, you're very good at that."

"I know," he replied in a smug tone. "I'm good at lots of things."

The look in his eyes was decidedly wicked. So wicked that Caitlin felt an answering flush creep over her body. Yes, there were several things at which Beau Collins excelled. Very little effort was required to remember how expertly his lips had coaxed a response from her. Was he thinking of that, too? She glanced away, hoping he couldn't guess how eager she was to have him kiss her again. Surely sophisticated women, the kind of women he preferred, didn't betray their eagerness so easily. But surely one glance from him didn't send blood pounding through their veins in the way that it was pounding through hers.

Beau continued to smile, enjoying Caitlin's pink-cheeked discomfort. She was as easy to tease as a high-school girl. Maybe easier. He suspected she'd been teased very little in her life. And why? What made her so different from everyone else he knew?

Their dinners arrived, and the flurry of activity gave her enough time to recover her poise. "Tell me about your teaching," Beau invited after they had made some initial progress on plates piled high with the specialty of the house, fried shrimp and hush puppies. "We've known each other for a while now, and I still don't know exactly what you do." She started to reply, but he stopped her. "Don't tell me—you're a history professor."

"Wrong. History is strictly a hobby," she retorted, laughing. "And I guess I assumed Hunt had told you that I teach at a private school, the Curtis Foundation. All my students are Down's syndrome children."

Surprised, Beau studied her for a moment in silence. "That must be a very challenging job."

"The challenge is worth it. My kids are special." Her eyes took on a soft, faraway look, a look Beau had never glimpsed before. That look transformed her in a way that no amount of makeup or glamorous clothes could.

Beau was intrigued. "Tell me about them."

She waved a hand in dismissal. "I don't want to bore you."

"You couldn't," he assured her. "Tell me. I really want to know."

Looking pleased, she began a halting explanation of her work. Beau pushed for details, and soon she had painted a vivid picture of the children who appeared to mean the world to her. A few of them stood out. There was Joey, the class clown. Beth, who had come further in two years than many children do in five. Billy, who loved to sing. And then there was Myra, who fought a variety of physical problems and still maintained a personality full of sunshine. Obviously this little girl was more special than all the rest.

Caitlin propped an arm on the table and settled her cheek against a cupped hand. "Myra reminds me so much of Julie."

"Julie?" Beau prompted, not recognizing the name.

Her hesitation was momentary. "Julie was my sister."

Beau supplied the rest of the explanation. Julie was like Myra, like all the children Caitlin taught. That helped explain why her teaching sounded more like a crusade than merely a career.

Eyes fixed on a spot somewhere above his shoulder, she anticipated his next question. "Julie died last year."

He didn't offer sympathy. No words could adequately address the loss in Caitlin's voice. She explained that Julie had suffered from problems with her heart ever since she'd been born, and finally, just two days after her seventeenth birthday, it had just stopped beating.

"She was in the kitchen," Caitlin murmured, shifting her gaze so that it met Beau's. "With Mother. Julie hadn't been feeling well, but she wanted some homemade cookies. It all happened so quickly that she was gone before an ambulance could get there." Still looking at him, she saw instead the utterly still and lifeless face of her little sister.

Beau spoke, his voice deep and smooth and oddly comforting. Caitlin blinked and realized she hadn't caught what he said.

"It must have been hard for your mother," he repeated.

Thinking of her mother, her mouth curved into the slightest of smiles. "Mother's strong. I believe she could handle just about anything. I'm the one who fell apart."

"And the rest of your family?"

"Aside from my cousin Walter, who's living in Australia, there is no family. My father left when Julie was two, and he died soon after that." There was no pain involved in speaking of her father. She knew nothing of him but the shadowed memory of a ten-year-old.

"So it was just you and your mother and Julie," Beau said, his expression thoughtful.

"Mother worked part-time while Julie was going to the school where I teach now."

"And what about you?"

"What do you mean?"

"What did you do?"

She frowned. "I helped with Julie, did chores around the house and went to school. What do most kids do?"

"I was just thinking that it couldn't have been easy for you. Your mother must have relied on you for a lot." He placed his hand over hers.

Caitlin shrugged. "I guess she did, but—"

"And how did that make you feel?"

Hesitating, she glanced down at the table where their hands were still joined. Aside from her mother, no one had ever bothered to ask how she felt about the demands Julie had placed on their family. No one. Not even Tom.

"I'm afraid I might have resented Julie," Beau murmured, almost to himself. "Didn't you?"

The protest that sprang to Caitlin's lips was reflexive, but she didn't give voice to it. With her mother she was used to denying any resentment. But with Beau the denial didn't seem so necessary. She had no idea why he was able to pull the truth from her, but telling him was easy, easier than she had ever dreamed it would be. "I did resent Julie," she whispered. "Not always and not for long. But sometimes." Surprisingly, that admission brought not guilt but a sweet feeling of freedom. It was good to tell someone how she really felt.

"Resentment is a pretty normal reaction, wouldn't you say?" As he spoke, Beau's gaze was steady on hers. Knowing about her family explained a lot about Caitlin. At a young age she had lost her father, and she had assumed some hefty responsibilities at home. It didn't take a genius to figure out that the household had probably revolved around Julie's needs, forcing Caitlin to grow up fast. No wonder she had developed such a serious outlook.

Turning from Beau's searching regard, Caitlin pulled her hand from his. He was easy, too easy to talk to. "I don't know why I'm telling you all this."

"And why not?"

"You couldn't possibly be interested."

His laugh was pleasantly deep, drawing her eyes back to his face. "If I wasn't interested, I wouldn't have asked you any questions."

She gave into a rueful smile. "You do have a way of steering conversations in the direction you want them to take."

"Watch out. I'll have you telling me all your secrets before the night is out."

"Maybe you should have been a psychiatrist."

He shook his head. "I'm afraid that would never have worked. I would have been compelled to ask questions in a bad German accent. You know, like, 'Is zere zomething you vant to tell me about zour mother?' I don't think patients would like that."

Their laughter rose and mingled, making for a pleasant harmony. On impulse, Caitlin again touched his hand with hers. "Thanks for listening. It must sound like my family is pretty mixed up."

"Every family has its problems."

"Like your problems with your parents?"

His green eyes, soft with laughter only a moment before, sharpened. "Why do you say that?"

She shifted uncomfortably in her seat. "You told me about them, on the beach. . . ." Her voice trailed away as she recalled what had happened after they had talked about his parents.

"You're right," Beau muttered, frowning. Up until now all he had remembered about that walk on the beach was the kiss he had shared with her.

"Maybe I got the wrong impression," Caitlin was saying, her eyes growing wide with concern.

He hastened to reassure her. "No, you've got the right idea. My parents and I don't exactly see eye to eye on anything."

"But surely they're proud of you."

He had to swallow a bitter laugh. "Why would you say that?"

"Well, you have your own business, you're successful—"

This time the laugh escaped him. "I will never be a success in my parents' eyes."

"But how can they—"

"Just trust me." His voice was harsher than he had intended. "My parents and I don't..." He stopped, realizing how impossible this was to explain to someone like Caitlin. She and her mother and sister had drawn together to help one another; his family had splintered. And his had never had desertion or illness or death to contend with. Everything he and his parents had ever quarreled over seemed trivial when compared to the situations Caitlin and her mother had faced. Compared to her family, his should have been a dream come true. Damn, but that made him angry.

Seeing that Caitlin still looked uncertain, he tried to make light of his feelings. "My parents don't approve of me or most of the things I do. Although," he paused, his eyes speculative as his gaze strayed over her, "they would definitely approve of you."

Her eyes widened even further. "Of me? Why?"

"You're intelligent and interesting and you have just the right sort of loveliness." He wondered, briefly, when he had formulated that description of her. It fit, however, fit very well.

Color brightened Caitlin's cheeks again, but she didn't look away, and she didn't protest the compliments. She wanted him to think all those things of her. "What kind of loveliness is the right kind?"

His voice dropped to a husky, intimate level. "The subtle kind. It blends with faded oriental rugs and the family silver."

"Do I do that?" she wondered aloud.

"Definitely." He was silent for a moment, watching her through narrowed but approving eyes. "Maybe I should take you to Chattanooga and match you to the rug and the silver tea service in the front room. Seeing me with you might even score some points with my parents."

"Is that important to you?"

The shake of his head was emphatic. "My parents' approval hasn't been important to me in a long, long time."

Caitlin wondered how that could be true. Anything that twisted his mouth so bitterly had to mean something to him. But she didn't argue with him, particularly since a teasing glint had replaced the ice in his eyes.

He signaled to the waiter for their check. "I'm not going to sit here all night when we could be having some fun. How about you?"

"It depends on what the *fun* is."

Looking smug, all he could say was, "Wait and see."

She envisioned dancing in the street or bar hopping, or something equally in keeping with his gregarious personality. What she didn't expect was a private, horse-drawn carriage tour of the historic district.

"We're leaving tomorrow night," Beau explained as he helped her into the carriage. "Even before I knew you were a history buff, I thought you'd enjoy some sightseeing."

The streets were dark and silent, nearly devoid of the tourists that had crowded them all day. Silvered by moonlight, the houses and gardens they passed were dreamlike flights of fancy. If one concentrated only on the moon and the steady clop-clop of the horse's hooves, it was easy enough to forget the distant sound of traffic and the smell of exhaust fumes. From there it was a simple step back into the past, and Caitlin lost herself in imagining the city as it had been more than a century before. She and Beau could easily be a wealthy cotton merchant and his lady on their way home from a ball where they had danced all night....

"I paid this guy to give you a tour," Beau whispered, his lips very close to her ear. "The least you could do is listen."

Caitlin straightened guiltily, realizing that she had been caught up in a world of her own. "I'm sorry, I was just—"

"Dreaming." Beau laughed and caught her hand in his own. Why was it he always seemed to be holding her hand?

"I'm sorry," she repeated.

"It's okay. There's no charge for dreaming."

"Really?" Her voice was soft, full of wishes. "I always thought dreams cost very dearly."

Her wistfulness was impossible to resist. And even if Beau hadn't spent days thinking of her lips, he would have kissed her. As it was, those days of waiting changed what could have been a soft, romantic kiss into something much deeper. Much more urgent.

*Why is it always an explosion?* he asked himself, even as his tongue begged her mouth to open to him. She complied, her lips blooming under his, inviting him in. Hot, moist, greedy, her mouth met every demand he made with one of her own. Who was the seeker, who the sought? He was no longer sure, no longer cared. There was no way to think when want was roaring through him with all the subtlety of a bomb.

On the seat in front of them, their guide's voice faded, dissolved into a cough and then changed to a cheerful, tuneless whistle.

Reluctantly, Caitlin pulled away from Beau. "We shouldn't be doing this," she whispered.

In answer he kissed her again. Kissed her until the driver's whistling and the pounding of her heart merged into one seamless flow of sound.

And this time it was Beau who broke the kiss. With hands caught in the soft glory of her hair, he groaned. "You know this is insane, don't you?"

She murmured her agreement against his mouth. The temptation was too much. He kissed her again.

"We have nothing in common, you know," she said when at last she was free again.

He nodded. "Nothing." The word was a sigh, again caught by her lips. With supreme effort, he moved away once more. "I never get involved with people who work for me."

"Then I quit."

His mouth captured her laughter, and they gave up all pretense of resistance. What could have been hours passed as they drove through the moonlight, ignoring the glories of old Savannah for the splendor to be found in each other's kiss.

But even the kindest of drivers couldn't circle the city forever. All too soon Caitlin found herself waiting in the hotel's courtyard while Beau paid their guide. What now? she wondered. A light came on in one of the inn's rooms, beaming across the dim garden. Her gaze drifted upward. If he asked, would she go to Beau's room? She started at a touch on her shoulder.

"It's only me," Beau whispered.

"Only you." Her voice trembled.

He drew her into the shadow of a tree, his arms slipping around her waist. Caitlin closed her eyes and tried to calm her jumping nerves with a deep breath. But the fragrance of flowers mingled with Beau's musky, masculine scent. Calmness eluded her.

His breath stirred the tendrils of hair on her forehead as he spoke. "Don't do that."

"What?"

"Don't tie yourself up in knots."

"Beau." She tried to move away.

"No." He held her steady. "There's no reason to be nervous. Nothing's going to happen that you don't want."

What she wanted was the whole problem. She wanted him, all of him, and that was more than enough cause for nerves.

"I know what I want," he continued in the same husky, arousing tone. "I want to make love to you. All night long. In every way you can imagine."

Emotion clogged her throat, preventing her reply. If his kisses had stirred her, they were nothing next to the potent caress of his voice.

His fingers feathered through her hair, down her cheek and across the kiss-swollen curve of her mouth. "But what I want isn't important. Not tonight. When I make love to you, Caitlin, I want to make sure it's as much your idea as mine."

"But Beau—"

"Ssshh." His kiss was gentle, undemanding. "When you want more, there's going to be plenty of time."

She could have told him then. Without words she could have lured him upstairs, and they could have spent the night in exactly the way he had described. What caused her to hesitate, Caitlin would never know. Maybe she expected the want to go away.

It didn't.

Even without the magic of moonlight and flower-scented air the want survived. When she opened her eyes to a gray, soggy morning, it was still there. Sharp enough to taste.

## *Chapter Six*

Frowning, Beau hung up the phone and gazed out the window of his hotel room. Raindrops ran down the glass, proving that weathermen were occasionally right. Below him, the garden looked dark, wet and singularly uninviting. Even the flowers had bowed to the rain's onslaught.

"Thank God we finished with the outdoor shots yesterday," he murmured, glancing at his watch. It was nearly nine. This morning they had a little more work to do inside the inn. Then Pete was going to spend the afternoon in the darkroom of a local photographer. Before they moved on to New Orleans, Beau wanted to be sure they had what they needed from Hilton Head and Savannah. Not that he had any doubt. Pete had never failed him. If only the same could be said for everyone.

His secretary had been on the phone, giving him the daily report. In the Knoxville office all hell had broken loose over the ad campaign for one of his other accounts. A smaller account, yes, but one whose needs couldn't be ignored. When the big guys had abandoned him, some people had remained loyal. Beau didn't forget loyalty.

Someone—either Molly or himself—would have to fly home and soothe some ruffled feathers. No doubt Molly could handle it. But it might be better if he left. Not better for the account in Knoxville. But better for the state of his emotions. Better for Caitlin.

He wasn't sure how or when she had gotten under his skin. First she had just been a face. Then she had been a challenge. Now she was an ache. But if he treated that ache with the obvious medicine, he feared the pain would spread. If he wasn't careful, even his heart could be affected.

"Impossible." The disbelieving word ripped from him. He wasn't going to put his heart in jeopardy with anyone. Particularly not with a woman so important to his business. Not even if she could hold him spellbound with a schoolteacher's tales. Not even if the touch of her lips took him to the edge of heaven.

*Or hell.*

Lord, but that was an apt destination. Where else could the entanglement of two such mismatched people be headed? He wasn't what Caitlin needed. He had a business to save, to rebuild. And yes, dammit, as much as he hated to admit it, he had something to prove to his parents. She didn't fit into his plans. While she was giving her life to a group of kids, he was jockeying for six-figure advertising budgets.

*They just didn't fit together.*

It didn't matter that in her presence he could forget his worries. It didn't matter that his laughter seemed able to chase the clouds from her eyes. All that mattered was that going any farther with their relationship was madness.

With that firmly in mind, Beau slammed out of his hotel room and collided with his partner in insanity. And madness became immediately appealing. Any man could be forgiven lunacy when confronted with the sight Caitlin made this morning. Her dress was short, and it clung to every curve of her slender body. Emphasized by that dress, her breasts looked to be a perfect fit for his hands. As for her legs—surely they were destined to slip around his hips. The potential for such insane and erotic encounters thundered through Beau's brain as he scowled down at Caitlin. *Where had she been hiding this dress?*

Blinking, she took a step backward. "I'm sorry. I didn't see you coming."

Still he frowned and didn't reply.

"Molly and the others are at breakfast. Are you going down, too?"

He ignored the tentative question and asked one of his own. "Are you wearing that for this morning's shoot?"

"Yes, Molly said—"

"Change," he ordered tersely.

"What?"

"Wear something else."

Caitlin's mouth thinned. He knew she hated it when he gave her orders. He couldn't say that he blamed her. He sounded like a marine drill sergeant. Clearing his throat, he tried for a lighter tone. "I don't like the dress, Caitlin."

"All right," she murmured, confusion replacing the resentment in her eyes. In an unconsciously alluring gesture she ran a hand down the curve of one hip. Beau followed the movement with greedy eyes. "Doesn't this look—"

"It looks damn good." His voice was as strained as he felt.

She straightened her shoulders, the motion thrusting her breasts tighter against the snug bodice. "If it looks good, then I don't—"

"*I* don't want you to wear the dress," Beau repeated, his voice tight, his loins tighter still. "Because if you do, I'm going to forget every honorable intention I've ever had." His husky tone dipped even lower. "And you're going to spend the morning in my bed."

His whisper clawed through Caitlin, and all she could do was gape as he strode away. With those simple, yet oh-so-complicating words, he awakened the want she had hoped to put to rest. Like a beast from the wild, this want had no respect for what was proper or sensible or possible. How could she have thought to tame a feeling so raw?

At the end of the hall, Beau turned back to her. "Did you say Molly was at breakfast?" Still dumbstruck, Caitlin nodded. "Good," he muttered. "I need to talk to her."

Caitlin shut her eyes, letting go of a deeply held breath. The unexpected sound of him saying her name snapped her to attention. Instead of walking away, he had retraced his steps and stood not an arm's length away, regarding her with his now-familiar, teasing grin.

He reached out, touching her chin with just the tip of his fingers. "Wear the dress, Caitlin." His fingers drew a straight line from her chin to the valley between her breasts. "But wear it in New Orleans. Just for me."

Beau left her then, cursing himself for his weakness. Molly was going to Knoxville. He was going to New Orleans. Where, no doubt, the insanity of his attraction to Caitlin would continue and reach its inevitable consummation.

She stood in the hall, hand pressed to the point where his touch had last lingered. It was so quiet, so still that the pounding of her heart seemed to fill the narrow space. Why hadn't someone told her desire could be like this? Devouring. Relentless. If she had known, she would have prepared for it.

Dimly, she remembered the passion she had shared with Tom Leland. How pale it seemed by comparison. It was hard to even remember Tom's touch when Beau's was so fresh. And as yet she hadn't even made love with him.

*Yet?* she repeated to herself. So it was a question of when, not if. She didn't know when that conclusion had been reached. In the carriage when he had kissed her? In the garden when he had said he would wait? Or a few minutes ago when his touch had scorched its way through her clothes? And what did it matter, anyway?

Feeling as if the walls were closing in on her, Caitlin fled to her room. Thankfully, Molly had not yet returned from breakfast. She had a few moments in which to assess the changes that had been wrought in two weeks. Only two weeks ago she had been fretting over what to do with her summer. Now here she was, contemplating an affair. Was this really her—planning *when* she would sleep with Beau?

Dazed, shaking her head, she turned and encountered her reflection in a mirror. A stranger looked back, the pretty, painted stranger Beau had created for his ad campaign. Caitlin scrubbed at her face with her hands, removing part of the glosses, the blushes and shadows that had become her stock in trade. But still, the woman reflected in the mirror was far different from the person she had known all her life. Where had that person gone?

Suddenly it seemed important to connect with someone who knew the real Caitlin. Hands shaking, she dialed the number of the University of Tennessee office where her mother had recently started working. Just the sound of Beverly Welch's husky, distinctive voice calmed her. The world stopped whirling as for a few moments they exchanged the ordinary, mother-daughter pleasantries.

Then there was a pause, and Beverly ended the chitchat. "Okay, Caitlin, are you going to tell me what's wrong?"

She grimaced. Fooling her mother had never been easy. "Do I sound unglued?"

"A little."

Since sex was hardly part of a normal conversation with her mother, Caitlin hesitated.

But apparently Beverly was more astute than even her daughter had realized. "It's Beau Collins, isn't it?"

A sigh poured from Caitlin, and just as effortlessly the whole story followed suit. Only she didn't tell her mother what she had intended. Instead of talking about the confusing emotions aroused by Beau's kisses, she found herself just talking about him. All about him. Nonsensical, unimportant details. His patience while she had tried to follow his and Pete's directions. His smile. The way he danced. His barely disguised bitterness whenever he spoke of his parents. His sympathy when she had told him about Julie.

"He's just...so..." Her voice broke on another sigh, and she settled back against the pillows of the bed. How did one describe perfection?

"And that's the problem?" Beverly asked, sounding amused.

"I guess..." Caitlin groaned. "I don't know."

Her mother chuckled. "It sounds as if you and he are becoming quite involved."

"Should we?"

Beverly laughed again. "Caitlin, dear, I hope you didn't call me in hopes that I'd tell you what to do. Because I'm not going to. You're a grown woman. You've been making—and living with—your own decisions for a long time."

"Like Tom," Caitlin said flatly.

"Yes, like Tom." To her mother's credit there was no hint of recrimination in her voice, although she had never liked or trusted the man. "I will tell you this much," she added with some spirit. "I certainly think Beau Collins is more your type than Tom ever was."

"My type?" Caitlin's voice squeaked. "That's a joke. The only reason he's interested in me now is because I'm playing this part for these ads. If I were just me—plain old Caitlin—he wouldn't be one bit interested."

"That's ridiculous."

"It is not."

"But Caitlin," Beverly protested, "you just finished telling me about all the things you and he have talked about. Would a man who's only interested in the way you look even bother with conversation?"

Caitlin was silent, considering that possibility.

"And speaking of the way you look," her mother added, "the possibility was always there. Just because you've gotten rid of those ridiculous glasses and put on a little makeup doesn't mean you're a different person."

"But, Mother, I feel so different."

Beverly's voice gentled. "Maybe that difference is because of some changes inside, as well as out."

"But I haven't changed."

"Haven't you?" Beverly sighed. "I've never heard you talk about anyone the way you talk about Beau."

"That's because I've never met anyone like him."

"And maybe he feels that way about you."

The idea seemed too preposterous to even think about. Caitlin's laugh was low and mirthless. "That's a pipe dream. To Beau I'm nothing more than a vacation romance. This will all come to a screeching halt when we get home."

"I swear," her mother grumbled. "No one would believe you were the same person who insisted that Julie was going to learn to tie her shoes. Do you remember that?"

"Of course." Caitlin would never forget those hours she had spent, endlessly tying and retying the laces of her younger sister's shoes. She had been so determined that Julie would learn to do that seemingly simple task. "Remember how proud she was when she did it?'"

"Remember?" Beverly chuckled heartily. "As I recall, we had a regular celebration. But what I'm wondering, Caitlin, is what happened to your determination. You used to fight for the things you wanted. If you want Beau Collins, why don't you fight for him?"

"Mother, it's not the same thing."

"Isn't it?"

For a moment there was silence between them, and Caitlin could imagine that her mother was pursing her lips, struggling not to say too much. She had never pushed too hard.

"Send me a postcard from New Orleans," Beverly said at last. "I've always heard it's a very romantic city."

"Mother—" Caitlin began in warning.

"Goodbye, dear."

Caitlin made a face as she replaced the receiver in its cradle. "Gee thanks, Mother, you really cleared it all up for me."

But her mother had given her a few things to think about. What *had* happened to her determination? Pushing her hair back from her face, Caitlin lay on the bed, staring at the ceiling. Faintly, she could remember those first enthusiastic days of her teaching career. She had planned to work miracles. Well, some people—including little Beth Holland's parents—would say she had. But it was never enough. Or so she had begun to think.

In all parts of her life, she had never been able to give enough. After all, if she had loved Tom enough, satisfied him, wouldn't he have stayed? As quickly as that thought surfaced, she backed away from it. Instead, glancing at the clock, she bounded off the bed.

She changed her dress, just as Beau had asked, and attempted to repair her makeup, although she knew Brenda would add something to her efforts. It was a little like playing make-believe, she thought, this dressing up for the camera. As a child, she hadn't had much time for games of fantasy. The demands of reality had been too insistent. Too real. But now—

Molly burst into the room before Caitlin could complete the thought. "I'm going to Knoxville," she announced, pulling a suitcase out of the closet. "Boy, have we got problems there."

Caitlin suppressed a grin, knowing the always organized, always clipboarded Molly dearly loved a good, challenging crisis.

"And you had better get downstairs," Molly added. "They're setting up." She paused and made a soft sound of regret. "I guess you'll be going to New Orleans without me."

*New Orleans,* Caitlin repeated silently. Even the name sounded enticing, like the creamy centers in a box of Valentine candy. Problem was, one piece was never enough. Even for sensible, controlled Caitlin. She had no doubt that Beau Collins would prove to be a similar, unrelenting temptation. Even if she didn't belong at his side. Even if the appeal she held for him was only make-believe. But maybe in New Orleans, in that magical delta of spellbinding romance, maybe there illusion could change to reality. Maybe in New Orleans.

*New Orleans.* The name put speed in her steps as she hurried downstairs.

Hot, moist and heavy, the city's summer air could choke you. On the worst days that air made movement about as easy as swimming in Jell-O. Even not moving required similar effort. Unfortunately, Beau thought, this was one of those days. Squinting, he glared at the sun and cursed the waves of heat rising from the sidewalk outside the New Orleans Plantation House inn.

Beside him, Brenda grimaced her agreement. "And we thought it was hot in Savannah. How foolish of us."

His attention focused on the scene Pete was attempting to capture, Beau murmured, "We're still fools." For only fools—or advertising men with a deadline—would be braving this late-afternoon heat. But at least he and Pete and Brenda could face the heat in shorts and T-shirts. Caitlin, in full antebellum regalia, stood sweltering beside the establishment's beautifully ornate door. Her smiling welcome didn't falter, even as she was asked to open the door again and again for the camera. Beau had to give her credit. No professional model could have handled this day with more aplomb.

Pausing only for a brief lunch and a change of wardrobe for Caitlin, they worked all day, moving in and out of the inn in an effort to avoid the heat as much as possible. After this shot and one more, Beau thought they would break for the day. After all, last night's rest had been extremely short.

Their plane, delayed by a thunderstorm in Savannah, had not landed in New Orleans until well past midnight. No hotel limousine had been waiting for them, delaying them further. It had been almost two-thirty before they had all been settled in their rooms.

And settled was perhaps the wrong word, Beau thought, rubbing his neck. Still another mix-up with the hotel had caused him to spend the night on a short, rather lumpy cot in the sitting room of Richter's private, third-floor suite. Caitlin had the bedroom,

Brenda and Pete had a room on another floor, but no provision had been made for Beau. The prissy little assistant manager had been most unaccommodating, making it clear that Beau should be grateful for even a cot. Tonight promised to be more of the same. Only if a guest with a reservation failed to show could the manager guarantee Beau a room with an honest-to-goodness bed.

Right now, with the sun blistering down on his head, he longed for that bed. The darkness of night. Cool sheets. A soft pillow.

And Caitlin.

And perhaps she was all he really longed for. Last night's narrow little cot might have felt like heaven if she had been in his arms.

Beau brushed dripping perspiration from his brow, wishing he could brush Caitlin so easily aside. Trying to concentrate only on what was happening before him, he moved to the side while Pete set up the shot from another angle. Caitlin followed their instructions without a word of protest, but her smile was a trifle wan. She looked tired from this angle, and her rapidly melting makeup couldn't hide the shadows under her eyes.

Perhaps she hadn't slept well, either, Beau thought, stopping the shot so that Brenda could do some makeup repair work. Had it bothered Caitlin that he had slept just outside her bedroom door? It had bothered him. He had lain wide-awake, eyes fastened on the brass doorknob glittering so enticingly in the room's semidarkness. He had thought about getting up, turning that knob, joining her. Wrestling with that impulse had disturbed his rest as much as his uncomfortable cot.

Having her had become an obsession. The desire was so intense that it was interfering with everything he tried to do. Even now, while he should have been thinking ahead to the next shot, he allowed himself to imagine Caitlin, her hair wild and loose on her naked shoulders, her slender body opening to accept him. Her eyes would be wide, stormy and darkened with passion, her breath catching in one of those almost soundless little sighs his kiss seemed to cause.

When? he wondered. Today? Tomorrow? He had told her and promised himself that he would wait until she was ready. But when? he asked himself again. His impatience swelled. The predictable physical reaction followed suit. And he swallowed the curse that rose to his lips. What was he doing standing here like this—hot and hard and hellishly frustrated?

Even as he asked the question, the temperature seemed to climb another degree, and he let loose with a particularly colorful, particularly loud stream of profanity. The words brought Brenda and Pete snapping around. Caitlin uttered an astonished little gasp, and unfortunately, so did the assistant manager who at that moment was heading out the door. The man's already thin nostrils pinched so tightly together that Beau wondered how he would draw a breath.

He managed, however, to begin a high-pitched, whining protest, "Now, Mr. Collins, we just can't have—"

Thankfully, his words were cut short by another gasp from Caitlin. But Beau's relief was short-lived as she turned a frightening shade of gray and swayed on her feet, grabbing the ornate grillwork covering the window beside the door for support.

"Caitlin!" Thrusting the manager aside, he caught her before she could slide to the sidewalk. Her face went white, and her body went limp against his own.

The ocean waves were cool. Refreshing, Caitlin thought, lifting her face so that the water could wash over her again. But why was it so dark? Where had the sun gone? Panicking, she fought her way up through the water and struggled to open her eyes as she broke the surface.

Gentle yet strong hands caught her, held her, soothed her. Who? she wondered. Then she heard the voice and she knew. At last she forced her eyes open. Beau. Sitting beside her in a chair. There were no ocean waves around her. Just cool cotton sheets.

"Welcome back," he said softly, leaning forward to switch on a lamp. Caitlin blinked as the light bounced off his bright, familiar hair.

"Where am I?" she managed to whisper, although her mouth felt as if it were lined with adhesive.

"This is your hotel room. I brought you up here after the paramedics left."

She swallowed, moistening her mouth. "Paramedics?"

His voice deepened with concern. "You don't remember the paramedics?"

Closing her eyes again, she lay motionless, enjoying the smoothness of the pillowcase beneath her cheek. She did remember something about men in white. With that memory, others came tumbling back. She had fainted beside the hotel's front door. Then she had been on a sofa in the hotel's lobby. Brenda and Beau had bent over her, and she had blacked out again. The men in white leaned over her after that.

"Remember?" Beau prompted. "They said it was the heat."

She opened her eyes then, suddenly remembering everything, including the way Beau had carried her to her room. She had been so weak, almost too weak to wash her face and take out her contacts. Brenda had been there, to help her out of that long, hot dress and into the gown she wore now. But it had been Beau who had sat on the bed for what had seemed like the longest time, stroking her face with a cool, wet cloth until finally she had drifted off to sleep.

Now, remembering his patient, unhurried touch, she studied him in thoughtful silence. "You didn't have to stay with me."

"Of course I did. I'm responsible for you."

She checked the protest that rose instinctively to her lips. At this moment, lying here, still feeling so weak and so weary, the thought of Beau being responsible for her was rather pleasant. Tomorrow she could again take care of herself. Tonight it was nice to know he cared enough to have stayed by her side. Judging by the darkness of the room, quite a while had passed since she had done her swooning act beside the front door.

"It's after ten," he said, accurately anticipating her question. He also stood and poured her the glass of water she was longing for. "You hungry?"

The thought of food was completely unappealing. "No." Caitlin pulled herself upright, surprised to find herself still lightheaded and swaying.

"Hey, take it easy." Reacting quickly, Beau was beside her on the bed, his arm slipping around her. "Here." He lifted the glass to her lips, and her hand came up, closing over his as she gratefully took a long drink of water. When she was finished he put the glass aside and leaned against the headboard, his arms still around her.

Quite naturally—or so it seemed to Caitlin—her head was soon tucked beneath his chin. She closed her eyes. He was so warm, so solid. Her arm slid around his waist as she cuddled closer. His hand strayed to the curve of her hip. This is as close to heaven as you get in this life, she thought, being held like this. In the silence she imagined she could hear his heart beating in rhythm with hers.

"You scared me to death, you know," Beau muttered, his voice rough.

"I guess I really threw a kink into the schedule, didn't I?"

"Who cares?"

"Molly would care. Her schedule is very important."

Beau explained in extremely graphic and rude terms where Molly could put her schedule.

Caitlin felt a smile tug at her mouth. "You seem to be rather fond of swearing today, Mr. Collins."

"It's been a tough day."

"Yes, it has." Smothering a yawn, she smoothed her hand up his side and across his chest. Beneath her fingers, against the thin knit of his shirt, she felt his nipple tauten. A groan, slight but distinct, escaped him. "Beau?" Tipping her head back, she saw that his eyes were closed and a frown twisted his lips. The frown deepened as she trailed her fingers down the center of his chest, down his belly, down to where the material of his shorts bunched at the juncture of his thighs.

He stopped her, his hand capturing hers. And for one long moment he held her there, so that she felt him harden, lengthen. Then, even as his lips lowered to hers, he drew her hand away.

"No—"

"But Beau—"

The protest was crushed as his mouth took hers. The movement was easy. Smooth. Like velvet against satin. And with the same whispering motion his tongue stroked deeper. Softer. Harder. Still deeper. The whirling rhythm spiraled in ever-widening circles. And the ache began. The wanting.

His hand, which until now had lain so chastely against her hip, edged upward, following the dip of her waist, coming to rest against the swell of her breast. And in imitation of the movement of his tongue, his fingers stroked the burgeoning nipple. Velvet against satin. Harder. Softer. Till the ache became deeper. The want even stronger.

And that's when he stopped, stopped kissing her, stopped touching her. It was moments before the eddying clouds of desire began to clear.

"Beau?" His name was more whimper than word as he edged away.

In answer he gripped her hand. Hard. And those dark, unexpectedly gold-tipped lashes of his swept upward, revealing eyes as green, as troubled as a rain-swept lake. With a sigh torn straight from the center of his soul, he pressed his face against the bodice of her blue satin gown.

"Beau?" The world was still twirling, but whether from desire or weariness she couldn't say. She felt heavy, too heavy to move.

Beau sat up and trailed a hand through her long, slumber-tangled hair. Sleepily, she smiled at him, and something—his heart?—turned over. What could he be thinking of to let things get so far out of hand? "Ah, Caitlin, you look like a little girl who's stayed up too long past her bedtime. How can I seduce a little girl?"

She only smiled again, her body curling next to his. Soft. Curving. Fragrant with the scent of flowers and feminine mystery. She was a woman, not a girl. A woman like no other he had ever wanted, a woman worth waiting for.

He eased away so that she could slide beneath the sheets once more. "When's the last time you got a good night's sleep?" he murmured, again pausing to stroke her hair.

"Since the first night you kissed me."

"Sorry about that." He grinned, feeling no remorse. "Go to sleep now. If you need anything, I'll be just outside—"

"No." Her eyes flew open. Her hand sought his. "Stay with me," she whispered. "Please."

He wavered. But only for a moment. A gentleman he might be, but he was certainly no saint. Only a saint would choose a hard, solitary cot over this woman's soft, welcoming bed. He switched off the light, tossed his shirt aside and slid in beside Caitlin. She moved into his arms with an openness, a trust that astounded him.

Sleep claimed her almost immediately, but it was a restless sleep, full of murmuring and movement. Hours passed. Time caught in the netherworld between torture and delight. Or so it felt to Beau. For there was both pain and pleasure in having Caitlin so near. Her legs were a silken, gentle weight moving against his own. The curve of her hip, the slight pillowing of her breasts were a temptation. He resisted and tried lulling himself to sleep by counting each of her sleep-softened breaths. It didn't work, and he lay for a long time with all of his senses fully alert, attuned to every shift of her body, flooded by the scent of her, nearly able to taste the honeyed sweetness of her skin.

Finally he must have slept. One moment he was floating, warm, safe and secure, and then the rumbling woke him. As he opened his eyes, the room brightened and then plunged back to the gray-edged shadows of dawn. Lightning, he thought. Beside him, Caitlin slept on. Moving carefully, trying not to wake her, Beau slipped from the bed to the bathroom. Then he went to stand beside the window.

The street below him was very dark, and another streak of lightning showed it to be deserted. The thunder rumbled, louder this time. Again the combination came. And again. Over and over. He didn't know how long he stood there, fascinated. A ferocious storm was brewing over the French Quarter.

"Beau?"

At Caitlin's whisper he dropped the curtains back across the window and turned to the bed. Lightning flashed again, and he saw that she stood in the doorway from the bathroom. When had she gotten up?

"It's going to storm," he whispered, and as if for emphasis, the thunder crashed, sounding as if it were directly overhead.

"Then come back to bed."

He took a deep breath. "Caitlin..."

"Please, Beau." Her voice was husky, deepened, he hoped, by need. "Come back to bed with me."

Lightning. Thunder. They collided inside him, sent him forward, toward her.

## *Chapter Seven*

Dreams. Everyone had them. Especially when it came to romance. Even Caitlin, in all her sane practicality, had lost some moments to wild, wishful thinking. Her dreams had always been an escape, a secret, safe place in which to hope for the unattainable. Secret, because she thought people as ordinary as herself should never be caught reaching for the stars. Safe, because she thought there was a rule about dreams never coming true.

It was only after inviting him to her bed that she remembered Beau didn't believe in rules.

He moved like the lightning. Quickly. So that he was at her side before it could thunder, before she could think. But perhaps that was good. Perhaps she had already wasted too much of her life on thoughts and worries and fears. All that really mattered was the taste of his lips, the strength of the hands that cupped her face.

The kiss was as it had been from the start, a dive into dark, enticing waters. There was no touching bottom. Not while his mouth was wet and hot and open against her own. Not while his tongue dallied so boldly with hers. Caught in a net of sensation, she surfaced in a steaming pool of want. The ripples spread outward, reducing her to a moist, heavy ache.

She moaned against his mouth, pressing closer. The crisp hair of his chest teased the skin left bare by the bodice of her gown. Eager for the feel of him, her hands moved up his back, savoring the play of muscles beneath his smooth skin. Her fingers trailed downward, coming to rest on his taut derriere, pulling forward until she could feel his erection nudging the gentle give of her belly. With a pleased sigh, she brought one hand around to tug at the zipper of his shorts.

*So much heat,* she thought, even as she cupped him.

Now the moan was his, caught in another flash of lightning, another peal of thunder. Her fingers moved against him, and he broke away from her mouth, his fingers tangling gently in her hair. "That sort of thing will get you in all sorts of trouble."

All her inhibitions lost to passion, she murmured, "I hope so," before pressing her mouth to the pulse beating at his throat. Here his flesh was hot, tasting of sun and the salt of honest sweat. His scent was the same. Musky. Unmistakably male. Lost in his flavor, she drew a circle on his skin with the tip of her tongue.

The sound he made was strangled, somewhere between sigh and curse. He swelled against her fingers, and hands that had lost their gentleness moved from her hair to her shoulders and down her arms, dragging the straps of her gown with them, tugging her hand away from him. The room filled with the zigzag of lightning, the boom of thunder. His lips dipped forward, catching hers as her gown slipped away from her breasts.

From there it was easy enough to get rid of the garment altogether. It slithered to the floor like a satin snake, coiling at her feet, joined by Beau's clothes. He kicked them aside, edging her toward the bed. Together they eased onto the sleep-tossed sheets. Then his hands were on her. Impatient. Then gentle. Then indescribably bold. He touched her with an artist's awe, stroking her to life. He touched her with a man's eagerness, fueling her passion. Beneath his hands, her breasts budded, tightened until the pleasure became pain, until she thought she might scream from the agony—or was it the sweetness?—of his touch.

Gasping, she arched her back. His kisses drifted down her neck and came to rest on her breasts. First one then the other. Lazily, his tongue worried the hardened tips, and all the breath seemed to press out of her lungs. While she struggled with that feeling, his hand dipped lower, across her stomach, inside the lace of her panties, until she helped him strip them away. The feel of his fingers on her, *in her,* brought a whimper to her lips.

"It's okay," he whispered against her throat, even as his fingers started their dance. "You'll see. It'll be okay."

Outside the rain began, pelting the balcony just beyond the window. In Caitlin's mind the sound melded with the touch of Beau's hand, the whisper of his voice. It all ran together. *She* ran together. Blood, bones, thoughts, prayers, everything inside her simply slid forward.

Thankfully, Beau was waiting to catch her.

He would have given anything to wait, just to watch her face as she skimmed from peak to peak and back again. But he had already waited what seemed like an eternity, almost too long. And so, with her name tearing from his lips, he brought their bodies together in one long, smooth thrust.

A cry of pleasure rose from deep in her throat, and her hips rocked off the bed, meeting him, her body melting around him. The contact was nearly his undoing. He waited, motionless, locked inside her, praying for the strength not to spill into her like some sailor on shore leave.

Then she moved. And shuddered. And called his name. And he was lost.

But thankfully, Caitlin was waiting to find him.

Twisting under him, arching upward, she came face to face with a dream come true.

Time ticked away as they lay together, breaths mingling, limbs entangled. Finally Beau rolled away, carrying Caitlin with him so that their positions were reversed. Outside the rain was ending, the thunder was only a distant rumble, and the darkness was lifted by the watery, pale light of dawn. He pushed the hair from her eyes, and waited, expectantly, for her to say something, anything.

She only smiled.

He settled her head against his chest and smiled himself.

At last Caitlin spoke, her voice a whisper against his skin. "You were right, you know."

"About what?"

"About waiting. Last night I was so out of it, I would have missed half of the good stuff."

He chuckled. "The good stuff?"

She raised up, her lips in a pretty pout. "Have you got a better word for it?"

"I guess not," he murmured, stroking a thumb across her bottom lip. She caught the thumb in her mouth, and he caught his breath. "It was pretty good."

"Only pretty good?"

Her tongue was moist against his thumb, moist and sexy as hell. Amazingly enough, he could feel himself tightening, stirring against the softness of her thigh. She felt it, too. He could tell by the way her eyes widened, darkened. Then she was moving up his body, her lips reaching for his, her hair a fragrant cloud that fell around their faces.

Before he could grow heavy with want, he drew back from the kiss. "I guess we're more than pretty good together."

"You guess?" She kissed him again, her laughter disappearing against his lips, reappearing when she pulled away. "You don't seem very sure of yourself this morning."

"Forgive me if I'm not thinking clearly. It's not easy to think when I'm in bed with a gorgeous, naked woman." He pushed himself up and rested on his elbows. Her long, slim legs—the legs he had dreamed of—slipped around his waist as she sat up. For a moment he contented himself with looking up into the dark hazel of her eyes.

"I knew it would be good," he whispered. His gaze flickered downward, beyond the hair curling over her smooth shoulders, coming to rest on her small, coral-tipped breasts. Fascinated, he watched those tips become hard, enticing pebbles. He grinned, his gaze flicking back to hers. She looked wanton, her mouth red from his kisses, her cheeks pink from the scrape of his beard. She bore only the slightest resemblance to the properly buttoned-up miss who had appeared at Pete's studio only weeks before. But enough of that prude remained for her to flush under his intimate study. Shyly, she crossed her arms over her breasts.

"Don't," he said softly. "You look so beautiful. The first time I saw you, I knew you could be like this."

"The first time you saw me I was holding a gun."

"That's right. And I figured any woman with that kind of guts must have some pretty spectacular depths."

"I see," Caitlin murmured, looking away. He uttered those superlatives so easily. Gorgeous. Beautiful. Spectacular. She was really none of those things. Especially as she probably looked now, with her hair tangled and her face wearing its pale, early-morning look. If Beau said she was beautiful then he was just seeing her as he wanted her to be.

"You don't see what I mean, either." He sat up, so that they were pressed together, torso to torso. "It isn't a matter of how you look, Caitlin. It's the way you are. Sleek and satisfied and sexy. It's exciting to know I made you look that way, *feel* that way. I like making you feel like that."

Oh, but he could make her feel a thousand different ways. With his kiss, full of passion and promise, he could make her anything he desired. She could believe anything, be anything when he held her. Being with Beau like this, naked and sated yet aching for more, could almost convince her that she was the woman she pretended to be.

For surely the old Caitlin wouldn't be in this bed. Surely she wouldn't be bold enough to press him against the sheets, to slip her body over his, to slide onto him with such abandon. Surely it was someone else who rocked so urgently against him, who met the arching of his body, who stared into his eyes as a storm shook through him for the second time that morning.

Later she lay silently at his side, spellbound by the afterglow of their joining. Moments like this weren't supposed to belong to people as ordinary as her. Were they?

But it felt so right. So natural to lie here with Beau, whispering lovers' secrets, watching the sun bring the day to life. She would worry about separating fact from fiction some other time. For now she would content herself with being what Beau imagined. There would be time enough in the future for her—and for him—to discover how radically she differed from that illusion.

Over breakfast she wondered if Brenda and Pete could tell how thoroughly everything had changed. They didn't appear to notice that she and Beau spent more time looking at each other than eating. No one dawdled over the meal. Beau wanted to hurry up and complete the two shots they had left undone yesterday.

"And then we're going to forget about everything and go play," he announced, squeezing Caitlin's hand under the table.

Pete paused, a forkful of omelet midway to his mouth. "What about the schedule?"

"To hell with it."

"Uh-oh," Brenda warned. "Molly wouldn't like that attitude."

"What Molly doesn't know won't hurt her," Beau retorted. "We've been working too hard. We deserve a little rest. Or else Caitlin will be passing out again."

"Beau, you're my kind of guy." Brenda tossed her napkin aside and pushed back her chair. "Let's get a move on. I'm ready to do some serious shopping."

Pete groaned and cast a dramatic look upward. "Heaven help New Orleans and my credit cards." However, he allowed his wife to drag him away from the table, pausing only long enough to grab a croissant and one last bite of omelet.

By noon, they were finished with the shots. Brenda, with a reluctant Pete in tow, went in search of bargains. Beau and Caitlin headed toward the river. He had promised her a Mississippi paddleboat cruise.

He insisted that they have the hotel limousine take them to the Riverwalk Mall where the boat departed. "I know that as a serious history scholar you would probably rather walk through the French Quarter," he said. "But I don't want you doing too much wandering around in this heat. You're probably still weak from yesterday."

Twining her fingers with his, she grinned. "If I'm weak, it's because of this morning. And you."

He brought their joined hands up to his mouth and pressed a kiss on her knuckles. "If you keep looking at me like that, the only memories you're going to have of New Orleans are going to be made in bed."

Teasingly, she dropped her voice to the same intimate level as his. "A day in bed sounds pretty good to me."

"Okay." Beau leaned forward. "Driver, you can turn—"

"Beau!" Caitlin protested, pulling him back. "I wasn't serious. I want to see the Mississippi."

"Are you sure?" he wheedled, leering comically. "We could do some serious cruising of our own. I promise to rock your boat and roll with your tide and—"

"Beau—"

"Hey, folks, what's it gonna be?" the driver cut in, his grin making it obvious that he had heard every word of their exchange. "Back to the hotel or to the river?"

Caitlin blushed crimson and sputtered, "To the river, please." Chuckling, the man turned his attention back to the road. Beau shook with suppressed laughter for the rest of their journey.

It wasn't until they reached the riverfront and were out of the cab that Caitlin felt uninhibited enough to protest. "You are impossible," she told him, her cheeks still flaming.

In response, Beau merely kissed her nose. "By now you should know better than to start anything with me in any type of vehicle. Remember what happened in the carriage in Savannah?"

"All right, all right," Caitlin said. He was impossible to resist when his smile was this broad, his eyes this merry. "Just try to behave on the boat, okay?"

He gave her his solemn promise, and all went well as they settled in shaded seats on the boat's middle deck. But Beau in a romantic mood was incapable of behaving himself. When the boat was passing through the port, he was kissing the edge of her shoulder. Jackson Square and a host of Victorian mansions drifted by while he was busy whispering a detailed description of exactly how he planned to make love to her next. Caitlin's face grew red, and the grandmotherly type seated near them snorted her disapproval and stalked off.

"See there," Caitlin hissed. "You're not only embarrassing me, you're making other people uncomfortable."

"She's just jealous," Beau murmured, trailing a finger across her jaw.

"Jealous?" It was hard to say anything when he touched her.

"Yeah." He leaned forward, his lips brushing against hers. "Secretly, I bet she wishes Grandpa still got hard every time he kissed her."

"Beau!" Involuntarily, Caitlin's eyes drifted down to the front of his shorts. How could he behave like this with a crowd of people around them? Everyone could probably tell what they were talking about. Was the lady standing at the rail staring at them, or was it her imagination?

His breath tingled against her cheek. "Let's find an empty bathroom and do something about this."

Caitlin squirmed. She hated to admit it, but his suggestion was tempting, so tempting that she was shocked at herself. Never before would she have entertained such a notion. But never before had she been with a man like Beau.

"What do you say?" he whispered again.

He couldn't be serious. *Could he?* It was impossible to judge by the look in his eyes, so Caitlin called his bluff. "Okay," she said, standing and pulling him to his feet.

"But—" Was that the slightest bit of hesitation in his voice?

"Come on." She drew him down the deck and through a set of swinging doors to the narrow corridor outside the ladies' restroom. A group of women passed them, their expressions curious, and then they found themselves all alone.

"I don't think..." Beau began, looking as if she had lost her mind.

"Who's thinking?" In one smooth motion, she pressed him against the wall, her mouth cutting off his last feeble protest. For a moment he simply reacted, his arms closing around her, his lips responding to the sensual pressure of hers. Then he recovered enough to push her away.

"Caitlin, for God's sake—"

"I thought this was what you wanted," she purred, twining her arms around his neck.

"But Caitlin—"

A chorus of giggles sounded behind them, and she peeked around to find several teenage girls watching in amusement. "Sorry, girls," she said. "But he's all mine."

"Caitlin—" Beau's voice had lowered to a growl.

The giggles echoed down the corridor as the girls disappeared.

Caitlin tugged at his arm, urging him toward the rest-room door. "Come on, I think the coast is clear."

He resisted. "Are you out of your mind?"

She grinned, and in a perfect imitation of the tone he had used earlier she said, "You should know better than to start anything with me on any type of vehicle."

Comprehension spread slowly across Beau's face. "Okay, okay, you've made your point. I will try to behave." He drew her back into his arms. "But just what would you have done if I had called *your* bluff?'"

"I guess we would have spent some time in the bathroom." Laughing up at his astounded expression, she twisted away.

He was in hot pursuit when they burst through the doors leading to the deck, and Caitlin collided with the older woman who had moved away from them earlier. The woman sniffed and muttered, "Absolutely shameless," before pushing around them.

"Jealousy is such an ugly emotion," Beau murmured as he guided Caitlin more sedately toward the rail surrounding the deck. In answer she drew back her head and laughed. Full. Uninhibited. Irresistible. God, how he loved hearing that laughter tumble from Caitlin. Smiling, he drew her against his side and stood silently watching the boat's paddle wheel churn the muddy river water.

She hadn't had enough laughter in her life. He was sure of that. Not enough laughter. Not nearly enough romance. Briefly, he allowed himself to speculate about the kind of man—or men—who had been in her life before. For she was no innocent. This morning had shown him that much. At least not innocent in the strictest physical sense of that word. Perhaps a better word would be *unawakened*.

He wanted to stir the passionate woman who slumbered inside her. He wanted Caitlin to know just how good it could be between a man and a woman. No, he amended that thought, he wanted her to know just how good it could be with *him*. *Only him*.

Feeling very possessive, he hugged her closer, and she tipped her head back to rest on his shoulder. Such a trusting gesture. And she was a woman from whom trust was not easily earned. Maybe that was his real victory, the real part of her he had stirred. The sexual response had merely followed. Because she trusted him, she opened herself to experiencing all he had to offer. And if he abused that trust, she would be hurt. Terribly so.

The responsibility was daunting, especially for a man who had never willingly assumed responsibility for any woman's feelings. Why was Caitlin so different? Why did she fill him with all these tender, protective emotions? Because of her, he was standing on the deck of a paddleboat instead of seeing to business. Because of her, he had, for the moment, pushed aside all thoughts of Dalton Richter's account. Forgotten were his agency's precarious financial position, his parents' certain satisfaction if Beau failed. Hearing Caitlin laugh had assumed far more importance than any of those admittedly pressing matters.

It occurred to Beau that he was slipping into dangerous waters. Perhaps he should be frightened. Perhaps if he stopped it now, he could do something about holding on to his heart. But perhaps losing his heart was exactly what he needed to do.

Deliberately, he pushed even the slightest thoughts of business and his parents aside. Instead, he concentrated on Caitlin, on making her laugh, seeing her smile, feeling her hand curl so trustingly in his. With the other tourists, they left the boat and explored the site of the Battle of New Orleans. Together, they enjoyed two of the boat's special frothy, tropical drinks. He succeeded in forgetting everything but the happy light in her hazel eyes. And his hold on his heart slipped even further.

Late afternoon sunshine was playing across the water as they disembarked, and still more lazy, undirected hours spun past as they wandered through the Riverwalk Mall, the French Market and toward the hotel. With the sun beginning to slide, the day lost some of its heat, but Beau still worried about Caitlin repeating yesterday's fainting spell. They took it easy, pausing to enjoy the music of a trio of guitarists in Jackson Square. He insisted on buying her a bouquet of flowers. He made her share a cup of rich, spicy gumbo with him.

"A before-dinner snack," he said. "We need to keep your strength up."

She laughed at his continued concern, but inside she filled with a secret warmth. She could get used to such caring attention.

Once back at the hotel, they forgot dinner in favor of making slow, sweet love, and Caitlin realized how easy it would be to grow used to everything about this man. He was a demanding lover, asking her to reach for heights she had never dreamed of scaling. He was tender, concerned for her feelings, putting her pleasure before his own. He was, as she already knew, mischievous, the sort of man who could sprinkle her body with petals from the roses in her bouquet and then make a lingering, sexy game out of removing each petal with his mouth.

He had many sides. Many more than the amused, unruffled, slightly indifferent facade he adopted for most of the world. Caitlin was well aware that he could manipulate a person with just a word, smiling all the time. The next morning, watching him do just that to the troublesome assistant manager of the hotel, she wondered about this side of him. There was an edge about him, a civilized but undeniably sharp ruthlessness. It showed when he wanted something, even something as simple as the movement of a few antiques in the lobby.

Frowning at that thought, she stood beside Brenda, watching Beau convince the manager to do as he wanted.

"Imagine what the State Department could do with a technique like his," Brenda muttered. "He could probably negotiate peace in the Middle East, and not one side would ever be able to tell they'd been conned."

For some reason the phrasing made Caitlin uncomfortable. "He is slick," she admitted reluctantly.

"And he's so nice about it." Brenda shook her head as the manager smiled and agreed to help. "What must it be like to always get what you want?"

The words further disturbed Caitlin. After all, she was one of Beau's victories. He had wanted her in this ad campaign, and she was. He had wanted her in his bed, and that was where she had spent the last two nights. What else would he want from her? Striving to sound unconcerned, she said to Brenda, "You make him sound very cold."

"Cold?" Brenda laughed. "Beau's not a cold person. You should know that better than most people."

Caitlin flushed and glanced away. So Brenda knew the turn her relationship with Beau had taken.

The other woman seemed to realize how her words had sounded. "Caitlin, I'm sorry. I didn't mean to embarrass you. But I've got eyes, and I know what's been happening between the two of you. I think it's great. Remember, I'm the one who told you to go for it with him."

"But now you make him sound like such a user."

"I didn't say that," Brenda insisted. "I said he knew how to get what he wanted. It's a talent, not a vice."

"Is it?"

Brenda rolled her eyes. "In business, you goose."

"So he doesn't use the same charms on women?"

"You are being silly," the blonde said. "Do you feel like you're being used?"

Did she? Until this moment she hadn't given it any thought. Caitlin thought back over the last few days. She remembered Beau's concern after she had fainted. He had sat beside her bed all evening. That hadn't been necessary. It wasn't as if she had been in any real danger. And as for what had happened after that...well, she couldn't say that he had used her. For goodness sake, he had stopped before anything could happen that night, even though she had made it obvious that she had no objections. Was that the action of a man who was using her?

Another, more unpleasant thought occurred to Caitlin. He could be trying to keep her happy so that the rest of the shoot would go well. She immediately resisted that idea. Beau might go to great lengths to get what he wanted, but she just couldn't believe he would go that far. To sleep with her in order to keep her happy? Preposterous. Besides, if he was so worried about the job, why had they spent most of yesterday playing?

"Caitlin?" Brenda prompted, clearly troubled.

At that moment Pete called for his wife. She gave Caitlin's arm a reassuring squeeze before hurrying across the lobby to help him adjust some lights. Caitlin glanced up, finding Beau's gaze upon her. He grinned. Her heart took flight. And all her doubts flew away, too.

"Come on, beautiful," he called. "Let's get this show on the road."

Maybe I'm the one who's using *him*, she thought, taking her place in front of the camera. For she would never find another man who made her feel as if she deserved these extravagant compliments. When this was over, she didn't know how she was going to go back to her rather drab existence.

But she couldn't think about drabness right now. Not that morning while she posed for the snapping camera. Certainly not that afternoon. For while Brenda and Pete were finishing up the last interior shots, Beau and Caitlin stole another afternoon for themselves. They intended to visit the zoo. They ended up in bed.

A tiny voice inside Beau's head reminded him of his responsibilities, reminded him that he might regret those hours if Pete switched a planned angle or missed some tiny but disastrous detail. But he ignored the voice in favor of more romantic pursuits. It seemed much more urgent to be with Caitlin, to watch her eyes grow slumberous with passion, to feel her hands sliding over his skin.

Their room was hot. One of them had left the draperies open, and the sun streamed through the windows with relentless intensity. The air-conditioning was making little impact. It was so hot that the budded flowers in yesterday's bouquet had opened wide and were dripping with fragrance. So hot that moisture beaded on Beau's forehead. So hot that Caitlin's white, silky slip clung to her body in damp patches. But it grew hotter still when they sank together to the sun-streaked bed. The sun had nothing on the wildfire they kindled.

In the quiet moments that followed their heat-soaked loving, Caitlin was in a confiding mood. Beau doubted that she intended to reveal so much about herself, but he learned a great deal. No one had ever made love to her in the afternoon. No one had ever taken her so far, so fast. No one had made her want to do the things they did together.

"This *no one* doesn't know what he missed, does he?" Beau whispered, watching Caitlin's eyes widen as she realized all that she had told him.

She dipped her face against his shoulder, but only for a moment. When she looked up, a smile was curving her lips. "I doubt that Tom would have thought this was the proper way to spend an afternoon."

"I'm glad he didn't."

"Oh really? Why?"

"I like being your first afternoon lover." Growling, Beau spun her on her back, pressing kisses down her throat.

Caitlin giggled. "You're crazy."

"Well, I can't have you lumping me into the same category with deadly dull old Tom, can I?"

"I assure you that will never happen."

"Good." He kissed her mouth then, long and hard and quite thoroughly. "In fact, I'm going to obliterate every memory you have of the guy."

"I've already started on that project," she murmured, pulling his lips back to hers.

He held back. "What possessed you to get involved with such a bore, anyway?"

Caitlin blinked and frowned, making Beau realize that he was prying. "I'm sorry," he said. "Tom is none of my business. Neither are any of the hundreds of men in your life."

A smile stole back across her face. "I can assure you there haven't been hundreds. And Tom was definitely the most significant."

"And he was dull?"

"But he was a brilliant teacher."

Beau raised an eyebrow. "Some smooth-talking, pipe-smoking professor, huh?"

"You should talk about smooth talkers," Caitlin retorted. "And you've got it wrong. Tom was a colleague."

He couldn't resist probing a little deeper, especially since she was still volunteering information. "He taught at the school where you teach now?"

She nodded. "He was wonderful. He worked a lot with Julie."

"Your sister?"

"Yes. He did a lot to help her grow more independent. He helped a lot of kids, but there were people who thought his methods were too offbeat, that he expected too much."

"Did he get canned?"

"No." She turned her gaze away from Beau's, and her eyebrows drew together, as if she was concentrating very hard on what she was saying. "Tom was—is—a loner, and I was a very temporary aberration for him. Someone he could argue theory and philosophy with. I thought that would be enough to hold him. It wasn't. He took a job in California." She paused and bit her lip. "He left right before Julie died." The simple words were filled with pain.

"That must have been hard to take all at once," Beau murmured, touching her cheek in sympathy.

"Losing Julie was so overwhelming that I barely noticed Tom was gone."

"Because it was really Julie who was the focus of your life." The words were a statement of fact, not a question.

Caitlin turned back to him, her eyes narrowing. Evidently, Beau had touched on a sensitive area. "She was my sister," she said slowly. "And I loved her."

"Perhaps more than would normally be expected."

"She was special."

Beau stroked a hand through her hair. "I know she was. I can hear it in your voice every time you talk about her."

"I know some people would think she was better off dead, that her death ended her struggles in life." Caitlin swallowed convulsively, her eyes filling with tears. "But those people never saw her face on Christmas morning. They never heard her singing to the birds outside her window. They never held her. They never got one of her extraspecial, super-duper hugs or..." She broke off, her cheeks coloring. "I'm sorry. I didn't mean to go off on a tangent."

"It's okay." Beau gathered her close in his arms. "I'd much rather hear about Julie than stodgy old Tom."

She laughed, a shaky sound, but a laugh nonetheless, and he held her even tighter. He knew then, even if he hadn't known before, that he was falling for this woman, falling hard. And if he had his way, her life would be full of laughter from now on. Laughter and kisses. Roses and silk. And afternoons spent like this one, making hot, steamy love.

Afternoon turned to evening, and reluctantly, Beau and Caitlin left their cocoon. She was sure what they had been doing all afternoon was written all over their faces. And she didn't care. If asked, she would have told the truth. If everyone knew how special Beau made her feel, then perhaps it would be easier to hold on to the magic.

She felt as if she had just come to life. Every inch of her tingled as they joined Pete and Brenda for a night on Bourbon Street. The famous avenue was thronged with people, bright with lights, alive with the sound of Dixieland jazz. They dined on shrimp creole, imbibed too much wine, wandered into several jazz clubs and wound up at a tiny, crowded café. There they lingered until the early hours of the morning, talking, laughing, drinking café au lait and eating crispy *beignets*.

Sighing over her second order of the sweet treats, Brenda said, "Now I feel as if I've really been to New Orleans. Bourbon Street, milky coffee and little square donuts. I can go home now." Everyone agreed, but it was with reluctance that they headed back to the hotel.

Caitlin suspected that, like herself, everyone was feeling a bit melancholy at leaving this city. Even with the thought of the morning flight to Atlanta hanging over her head, she didn't want to go to bed. She felt like a kid again, trying to hold on to the last days of summer. Beau indulged her, holding her close in the darkness while she chattered on about a hundred and one inconsequential matters. But soon his breathing relaxed into the even cadence of sleep, and still she lay awake.

They had three more days of work left. Three days and then what? What could follow the magic of this city? Today she had mailed her mother a postcard. "You were right," she had written, "New Orleans is romantic." Knowing that tidbit would only tantalize her mother, she had dropped it into the postal slot at the front desk and laughed. Now she didn't feel so happy. When they were back on familiar territory, away from luxurious rooms and romance-laden streets, would Beau still want her?

She shut her eyes, trying to ward off the feeling that everything was drawing to a close. Finally she fell into an uneasy sleep.

The unease was still there when she woke the next morning, roused by the shrill ring of the telephone. Blinking, she watched Beau grope for the receiver, heard him answer, saw him sit up abruptly and switch on the light.

"Mother?" he said, his deep voice full of disbelief. "What's wrong?"

## *Chapter Eight*

Another van. Another drive to another hotel.

As they headed from the airport to the Plantation House Resort just north of Atlanta, Beau wondered if he'd ever again feel quite the same about traveling. What had once been a favorite pursuit now seemed an unending, exhausting transfer of luggage, equipment and people. Right now he would like nothing more than to be at home, putting his feet up and watching a movie with Caitlin.

Home. Where was that anyway? He had an apartment in Chattanooga that he rarely saw, an apartment in Knoxville that wasn't even his, and his parents' house had ceased to feel like a home a long time ago. For years now his entire focus had been a rootless scramble for success. He wasn't so sure that was what he wanted for his future. If he didn't watch it, he'd end up with a life as narrow in focus as his father's.

Beau leaned his head against the window, thinking about his father. Judging from the conversation he'd had with his mother this morning, the man was going to have to make some adjustments in his life. Big adjustments. He wouldn't like that, but according to Beau's mother he had no choice.

Frowning, Beau remembered the sound of his mother's voice. She had sounded...well, the only way to describe her voice was weak. And she had never sounded that way. Not to Beau. It was as if at hearing his voice, hers had failed her. That was why he had immediately known something was wrong.

"It's your father," she'd murmured faintly.

The fear that had squeezed through Beau had surprised him. "What's wrong with Father?"

"There's nothing...I mean..." His mother had cleared her throat, and her voice had strengthened. "I don't want to upset you, Beau. Your father is fine now. But yesterday he had a...a spell."

"Spell?"

"He's exhausted," she explained, sounding more like herself by the moment. "You know how he works. And it's all just caught up with him."

Beau couldn't imagine his father laid low by anything, especially his work. He lived for the intricacies of litigation. "Is he in the hospital?"

She laughed, a mirthless sound. "Are you kidding? He wouldn't stay in the hospital. He's here, at home. He's taking a few weeks off, and he's promised me he's going to turn more responsibility over to someone else. Dr. Amherst said this was just a warning, that your father's body is telling him he has to slow down."

"That'll be the day," Beau muttered. "He'll die in that damned office of his."

At his mother's soft cry, he instantly regretted the words. "I'm sorry," he replied automatically, amazed by this never-before-seen side of his mother. She had always been so in control. "Do you want me to come?"

She hesitated. "I don't think that's necessary. I mean, I know you're working. That girl of yours—Maggie?—"

"Molly?"

"Yes, Molly. Well, I found her at your office late last night. She told me where I could reach you. She said you're working on some important project—"

"Mother, I can get away if you need my help with Father."

Another pause. "I can handle your father."

A tactful way of saying I'm not needed, Beau thought with the familiar bitterness. "No doubt I would just upset him more."

"Now Beau—"

"Is there anything I can do, Mother?" Her silence stretched even longer this time. "Mother?" he prompted.

"I just wanted you to know," she said at last, and her voice held that curiously broken sound again. "I didn't want Melissa calling you up and telling you, upsetting you. No doubt someone from your father's office will tell her—everyone eats lunch at her restaurant. Your father said I wasn't to call you, that you were busy and that he was fine. But I . . . I just wanted you to hear it from me."

Beau had held the phone, surprised by his mother's concern for his feelings. Such thoughtfulness was an interesting development. While he'd been in college, she had gone into the hospital for an emergency appendectomy, and it had been two weeks before he'd been told. They had said they didn't want to distract him from his studies, but Beau had been hurt. Why was this incident with his father any different? What was happening? First the show of affection when he had visited last week. Now this. Could it be his parents were mellowing?

Impossible, he thought now, just as he'd thought this morning after his mother had hung up. It was impossible for his parents to change. Wasn't it?

With that question nagging at him, he turned from the window and studied Caitlin. She was curled on the seat beside him, sleeping. This morning she had also been beside him, and she'd had only one question when he'd told her about his father.

"Are you going home?" she'd asked.

He had shaken his head, and her sleepy eyes had grown round with astonishment. He knew without a doubt that given the same situation, she would have gone instantly to her mother's side. He envied her that sort of simple familial devotion. His feelings for his parents were just too damned complicated.

But now, watching Caitlin sleep, Beau knew with certainty that he had one relationship that wasn't beset by doubts or complications. He loved Caitlin. Loved her—simple, unqualified love. He didn't know when he had made the decision, but the nebulous feelings that had been welling up in him now had a name. Love. He loved Caitlin.

This wasn't the way he had expected it to feel. Somehow he had retained the adolescent notion that when the real emotion hit him, there would be bombs bursting, flags waving and crowds cheering. He certainly didn't expect the realization to be so subtle, or for it to come as he rode down the interstate with the woman of his dreams sleeping beside him. But like the gentle spread of warmth from a fireplace, the feeling rolled through him.

*He loved Caitlin.*

It took all of his control to keep from rousing her. He couldn't tell her. Not now. Not any time soon. They had known each other less than a month, and he knew that her sensible mind would reject the possibility that what he felt was genuine. To tell her now would drive her away. No, he had to wait. They could settle into some sort of pattern in Knoxville. They could date and really get to know each other—the day-to-day kind of knowing that only time can bring. Then, after all his business problems were cleared—

Business problems. The agency. Dalton Richter. For the first time in days, Beau spared those problems more than a passing thought. Of course, he had spoken with Molly several times, including this morning. She had smoothed over the incident with the client in Knoxville, and as usual she seemed to have everything under control. While he had been away, an account executive had cemented the agency's relationship with another small but prestigious account. Several other accounts had—thank God—paid their bills. Now if everything worked out with Richter, the agency would be fine. They would win other accounts. He could give Molly and the rest of the loyal staff well-deserved raises.

He could make it, he thought, filling with resolve. He was still going to make the agency into a southeastern powerhouse. But it wasn't going to be his whole life. He wasn't going to live as his father had. He wasn't going to ask Caitlin to take second place to any business. Beau was going to have it all.

What a nice fantasy that was. And it could be his. Someday he'd have a home, a wife, a family. His business would be rock-solid successful, so successful that his father would enjoy boasting of his son's business prowess down at the club. The success would be *Beau's*, in the field *Beau* had chosen, but the approval would be *his father's*.

The van changed lanes, rousing Beau from his daydream, and the bubble burst. Impatiently he chastised himself. Why couldn't he forget about his parents and learn to please himself? For as long as he could remember, he had been trying to march to his own drummer *and* dance to his parent's tune. It was an exhausting effort. But he had to do it. He had to show them something. Didn't he?

Caitlin stirred and lifted her gaze to his. She blinked and looked around. "Are we there?"

"It shouldn't be much longer," Beau assured her. "Go back to sleep."

She stretched, looking for all the world like a lazy, contented cat. "No. I'd better wake up now." Some of his agitated thoughts must have communicated themselves to her, for she turned her thoughtful gaze to Beau. "Is anything the matter?"

She's already learning to read me, he thought. Oddly enough the idea didn't threaten him in the way it once would have. It might be good to share some of his burdens with Caitlin. But not right now. Not when the realization of his true feelings was still so new. Not when all he really wanted to do was slide his arms around her. He followed that impulse and assured her that nothing was wrong.

Caitlin didn't believe his assurances. She knew something was troubling Beau. Perhaps he was worried about his father. And then again, maybe not. This morning he had shaken off the news of the man's collapse without batting an eyelash. She really shouldn't have been surprised. Over these last two weeks, he had told her something of the sort of relationship he had with his parents. But surely in the face of illness they could put their differences aside.

She would have liked Beau to share what he was feeling with her. But she didn't push. If she had learned anything about him, it was that that cheerfully blasé mask of his couldn't be cracked. Oh, he allowed a peek behind it now and then, but only when it was his idea. She could only hope that would change the longer they were together.

Longer? Now that was dangerous thinking. If she was wise, she wouldn't let her thoughts go any further than tomorrow or perhaps the day after that. When they got back to Knoxville everything could and probably would change. The uneasiness that had hampered her sleep last night returned in full measure. This... this *fling* could be over very soon. Then what would she do?

Before such unsettling thoughts could take over, Caitlin drew a steadying breath. She wasn't going to bother with those eventualities right now. She knew she was thinking in a very Scarlett O'Hara-ish fashion, but she didn't care. She would concentrate on what the moment was offering. And right now the moment offered her the comfort of Beau's arms and through the windows of the van, her first glimpse of another Plantation House Resort.

Like Hilton Head, this resort was fairly new. It shared a similar layout, too. But where the ocean had formed the backdrop before, this time there was a shimmering lake. At the center of the resort was a white plantation-style building that sat on a rise of land overlooking the water. The building was not so new that ivy had not already begun its climb up the sides. White columns supported a two-story veranda, and inside was all the cool comfort and genteel hospitality one would have expected of Tara, Scarlett's legendary home. How appropriate for my state of mind, Caitlin thought, following the others inside.

The lobby, registration desk and other offices occupied the first floor. A pretty assistant manager, as agreeable as her counterpart in New Orleans had been cantankerous, explained that the second floor was given over almost entirely to a restaurant and lounge. Taking the wheel of the van, she conducted a tour of the grounds as she escorted them to their condominium.

A clubhouse boasted another restaurant and lounge. There were two swimming pools, a golf course and several tennis courts. Vacation chalets and condominiums had been built among the tall pine trees that dotted the slope down toward the lake. There, trucked-in sand had created a comfortable beach, while on the shore nearest the main building were twin piers where motorboats could be docked and sailboats rented. As Caitlin had learned to expect from Plantation House Resorts, there were flowers everywhere, in well-tended beds, spilling from boxes and baskets, scenting the air.

"We're booked almost solid because of the holiday," the young manager said as she unlocked the door to a chalet near the lake. "But we managed to save some of our best accommodations for you." She winked. After showing them through the comfortable three-bedroom cottage, she turned to leave but checked herself at the door. "There'll be fireworks at ten tonight. You might be able to get some good shots for the brochure." With a last friendly smile, she was gone.

"Is it really July 4th?" The last few days had passed in such a blur, Caitlin had lost track of time. Sighing tiredly, she sprawled on the sofa that bisected the large room. The tweedy, overstuffed cushions gave pleasantly under her weight. It would nice to stay right here for a couple of hours.

Brenda followed Caitlin to the sofa and affected a dramatic, long-suffering pose. "Oh yes, it's a holiday. And here we are—chained to camera and tripod, condemned to spend what's left of the day working."

Merely smiling at the Brenda's remark, Beau loaded himself down with several of Caitlin's suitcases.

"Well," Caitlin demanded of him, "are you going to be unpatriotic and make us work?"

"Sure am," came the cryptic response as he started toward the bedroom that branched off one side of the room.

"But I'm exhausted," Brenda complained. "Caitlin's worn to a frazzle, and Pete . . ." she paused, suddenly realizing her husband wasn't anywhere to be seen. "Where is Pete?"

Pausing, Beau nodded to the opened glass doors that separated the living room from a deck overlooking the lake. "Looks like Pete is already at work."

Caitlin and Brenda swiveled around. Sure enough Pete was on the deck, attaching his camera to a tripod.

Exhaustion forgotten, Brenda bounded from the sofa, calling, "Peter Brian Foley, can't you even shut a door? There's air-conditioning on in here."

He turned to her with the expression of a man summoned from another world. "But honey, would you look at this light—" The door Brenda tugged shut behind her reduced his protest to an unintelligible mumble.

Laughing, Caitlin pushed herself up from her seat. "They're a perfect match," she said, nodding toward the couple on the deck.

Beau grinned. "Yeah. Pete has an artist's cockeyed view of the world. Brenda's head is level and screwed on very tight."

"They complement each other well."

"So could we."

The quietly spoken words brought Caitlin's gaze spinning around to meet Beau's. She swallowed and tried hard to adopt a nonchalance she didn't feel. "Could we?"

"Yeah." His smile spread all the way to his eyes. "We'd make a great team if you'd just get over here and open this door before I drop all these bags. What's in these, anyway, lead?"

A little embarrassed by the significance she had mistakenly read into his teasing words, Caitlin hurried to open the door to the bedroom, grumbling, "It's just like a man to try to carry all the bags at once."

"Just like a man," Beau mimicked, following her inside and dropping the cases near the room's king-size water bed. Then, without ceremony, he tumbled Caitlin back across the bed, smothering her protest with a scorching kiss. He raised himself up, and his thumb stroked across her trembling lower lip. "My goodness," he whispered, "imagine how nice and calm and uneventful life would be without us men around."

In answer, Caitlin drew his lips down to hers again.

"You could at least close the door." The giggling admonition drew them apart several minutes later, and Caitlin looked up to see Brenda and Pete grinning at them through the bedroom's open door.

In answer, Beau got up and slammed it shut.

"What do you say we work a little on our complementary styles?" he suggested, sliding across the gray satin comforter toward Caitlin.

At just the heated look in his eyes she could feel the excitement winging through her, a quickening of her pulse, a strumming ache between her thighs. But she felt duty-bound to resist a little. "And what about work?"

"You've got to get undressed, anyway, to change for this afternoon's schedule," he reasoned, his hands already undoing the buttons of her blouse.

One minute he was grinning, practically teasing her out of her clothes. The next she was naked beneath him, her body opening in welcome. How did he do this? she wondered. One touch from him, and she forgot the couple on the other side of the bedroom door, forgot everything but sensation. The cool satin beneath her. The taste of his skin. The pull of his mouth moving against that most intimate juncture of her body. She supposed she was bewitched, caught in the sexual spell that Beau could conjure up with just a flicker from his green eyes.

She could feel those eyes on her for the rest of the day and night. In a white muslin dress resembling Scarlett's famous picnic attire, she posed on the veranda of the main building. A curious crowd gathered to watch, but it was only Beau's gaze that she felt. In the clinging red dress he had objected to in Savannah, she danced in the glass-enclosed clubhouse lounge. The hired model she moved with was handsome, but it was Beau's burning gaze she returned to again and again. She blew the shot so many times that even Pete's long-lasting patience threatened to snap.

Finally the night's work was finished, just in time for the fireworks display to begin. Multicolored starbursts twirled through the sky, ending in a rainbow hail of lights, earning oohs and ahhs from the crowd. Yet Caitlin didn't find those colors any brighter than the ones Beau's touch could arouse inside her.

"Brenda and Pete will think we're shameless," she whispered as they hurried through the pine-scented trees to their chalet.

"Does what they think really bother you?"

She squeezed his hand. "Not enough to turn back."

"Then let's go."

Though there was urgency in his voice, he didn't hurry once they were at the chalet. Instead, he drew Caitlin out onto the deck, and she stood in his arms, leaning back against his broad chest as they watched the fireworks. They were close enough for the flares to lighten the deck, but far enough away to feel as if they were the only people on earth.

His words, after a long silence, surprised her. "After we're through here, I'd like you to come to Chattanooga with me. Could you?"

She turned, wishing there was enough light to read the expression in his eyes. "Do you want me to pose—"

"No." The word cut her short, and he cleared his throat. "I'm going to visit my parents for a while, make a long weekend of it."

"But with your father not feeling well, won't it be an imposition?"

"Are you kidding? They'll be thrilled to meet you." He laughed. "I told you before. My parents will like you."

A tingle of uneasiness moved down Caitlin's back. What had Beau told her that night at dinner in Savannah?—that his parents didn't approve of anything he did, but that they'd like her. Somehow, she doubted that. Parents who could rent a seaside cottage for a summer or think of sending their son to an Ivy League school would want more for their son than Caitlin Welch, teacher and pretend model, an imposter in glamorous clothing.

"Will you come?" Beau pressed. "I think it would do my father good to have some company. And I really want them to get to know you."

The warmth of those words was Caitlin's undoing. If he wanted her to meet his parents, surely that meant he was thinking of her as something more than a casual affair. Surely. The hope sent her pulse fluttering. "Maybe you should call your mother before we suddenly appear on her doorstep."

Beau had been thinking of just such a surprise attack, but he nodded his agreement. Anything to get Caitlin to go with him. He longed to take her into that house, to see his parents' faces, to know he had done something of which they could approve. For they would approve of Caitlin. Who would ever have guessed that he'd fall in love with a woman so appropriate?

So appropriate. And so damned sexy.

He took her into his arms again as a particularly bright rocket split the night sky and fell, bathing her in a splash of cascading colors. In that brief brilliance, his attention was caught by her mouth. Softly curved. Tempting. God, so tempting.

"Let's go inside," he murmured. "Before the others decide to come back."

In the room they were sharing, the bedside lamp had been left on, and beyond that pool of light, Caitlin moved to take off the clinging red dress. Beau stopped her. "Leave it," he whispered.

She turned to him, confused. "But—"

Gently, he drew her back to the light. Through the second skin made by the fabric, his hands traced down her body. His thumbs paused, drawing circles around her breasts until her nipples were taut and well-defined. Then his hands slid further down, intent on their exploration. Over her stomach. Around to the curve of her bottom. He said nothing. He just touched. As if he had never touched her before.

Maybe it was the brush of the dress against her flesh, but Caitlin's arousal was sharper, harder than if she had been naked. She stood silent, trembling, wanting to touch him but afraid to break the enchantment of this moment.

Finally, he kissed her, and she found herself being pressed down on the bed. His lips retraced the path his hands had taken, caressing her through the dress. Then his hands tugged her skirt up, and with agonizing slowness stripped her hose and underwear away.

Need, like a forbidden drug, whispered through her veins.

She *had* to touch him. Her hands found the hard muscles of his chest, the cold metal of his belt buckle, his zipper, the heavy maleness of him. Perspiration pooled in the valley between her breasts, beaded behind her knees and dampened her temples.

And still Beau said nothing. He touched. And touched some more.

At last, when his silence had assumed an eroticism all its own, he spoke. "You were supposed to wear this dress in New Orleans. Why didn't you?" The husky whisper seemed to curl over her skin, and beneath his hands her body jerked, at the very edge of climax.

"Why?" he whispered again.

She couldn't risk an answer. There wasn't enough room in her lungs for the breath speech would require.

"I'm glad you waited." His words were a sigh, murmuring across her senses. His hands were lighter still, pushing her dress up around her waist. Then he filled her, and they rocked together toward oblivion.

The pleasure was unspeakable. It left Caitlin shy, almost afraid to meet Beau's eyes. He, however, would have none of that reticence.

"Look at me," he whispered, lifting her chin with his fingers. "That was incredible." His lips nibbled at hers. "You are the sexiest woman alive."

She flushed at his exaggeration. "Beau—"

"You are," he insisted. "Every time with you, it gets better."

Pushing her dress down over her hips, she moved away and sat up. She felt disoriented, as if she had fallen asleep in an unfamiliar place. Turning, she met

Beau's gaze. His eyes were deeply green, still filled with warm promise.

"I've never wanted anyone the way I want you," he said.

He couldn't mean that, Caitlin thought. This was all some sort of dream. Beau must have wanted—and won—a dozen women more desirable than she. Although surely desire sharper than what they had just experienced was impossible. She shook her head, more to clear her thoughts than to deny anything Beau had said.

He swept her back down beside him. "It's true," he insisted. "I want you so much that there's a point when you could ask me to do anything."

Was there? That intrigued Caitlin, who had spent so much of her life feeling as if she had no control over events or people. She couldn't help smiling. "I sort of like knowing that," she admitted.

The simple assertion of power seemed to please him. He grinned and kissed her nose. "In fact, at this moment, if you asked me to go hunt down a hot fudge sundae, I would probably do it. Even though I'm in an extremely weakened state."

"I didn't say anything about a hot fudge sundae," Caitlin said, amused.

"You didn't? A few minutes ago I could have sworn you moaned something about fudge."

She giggled. "I think that was you. Do you want a hot fudge sundae?"

"I'd kill for one. Hot sex always makes me want hot fudge."

"Then let's go find some."

Pausing only to make themselves presentable, they went back out into the night. And somehow Beau bribed a young waiter in the main lounge to find them some ice cream. He couldn't, however, locate any hot fudge.

"This is the best I can do," he said and presented two dishes of chocolate ice cream with a flourish.

"I guess it'll have to do," Beau muttered, looking truly disgruntled. "But this cuts your tip in half." Amazed, Caitlin saw him press a twenty dollar bill in the kid's hand.

Twenty dollars for two cups of ice cream. It was exactly the sort of ridiculous thing Beau would do. And it was exactly the reason she loved him.

Yes, she loved him. She could admit that to herself even as they took their ice cream down to the veranda. She loved him for all the reasons she had first resisted him. Because he had a glib answer for everything. Because he made her feel things she didn't want to feel. He was crazy enough to sneak in a strange bathroom window. Tender enough to sit by her bed for hours. The man in him could take her to the stars. But there was enough of the boy left inside for him to wish for ice cream at midnight.

She had to love him. For where could she find another man who could make her think, make her laugh, make her feel? For her there would never be another man like him. He was her one chance at having it all.

But how to hold him? Caitlin had no idea. They had something between them, yes. A strong sexual pull. But she didn't delude herself on that score. Sex would never cement any relationship. Sex without love was like the taste for ice cream on a hot summer night, you eventually had your fill. If she and Beau were to have something that lasted, he would have to love her, too.

As had become her habit recently, Caitlin decided not to agonize over what she didn't know how to change. "I'll worry about love tomorrow," she said as she faced her reflection in the bathroom mirror the next morning. Tomorrow, her modeling job would be over. That would be soon enough to return from the real-life fantasy she had been living.

That day's work went well. A pose down by the sailboats. A shot each in the lobby and restaurant. A few hours outside by the pool, on the tennis court and golf course. The heat wave that had gripped the South for the past few weeks had eased, and the work went faster. By seven o'clock that evening, Caitlin was finished. Tomorrow, Pete had a few wrap-up shots to take. Then he and Brenda would fly back to Knoxville. Caitlin and Beau were renting a car for the drive to Chattanooga.

In celebration of a job well done, Beau ordered champagne with their dinner. They popped the cork and exchanged toasts in the clubhouse restaurant.

"To romance," Brenda proposed, her blue eyes merry as she touched her glass to Caitlin's.

Pete rubbed at his shaggy beard. "That's an unusual toast."

Brenda winked at Beau. "Not really."

"No, not at all," he agreed, passing the wink on to Caitlin.

"Yes, to romance," she echoed.

They all drained their glasses, and spent the next few minutes laughing at Pete's still-bemused expression.

Leaving Brenda at the table to explain the dynamics of the situation to her husband, Beau drew Caitlin onto the dance floor. The restaurant had hired a local jazz combo for the evening, a group of older musicians who specialized in the melting rhythms of George Gershwin and Cole Porter. It was music made for dancing, and even the younger people in the crowd were responding to the mellow mood.

It was certainly the right music for Beau's frame of mind. He was feeling immensely relieved. The photo shoot was over, and he had no doubt that Richter was going to love the results. Tomorrow, Beau could take Caitlin to meet his parents without worrying about anything. And beyond that... well, to coin a corny phrase, he thought this was the beginning of the rest of his life. Sighing happily, he laid his cheek against Caitlin's soft, fragrant hair.

"So nice to see you both enjoying yourself."

The booming voice could belong to only one person. Especially as it was accompanied by a white suit and a cloud of cigar smoke. Halting in midstep, Beau turned and found himself face-to-face with Dalton Richter.

## *Chapter Nine*

Mr. Richter," Caitlin murmured, glancing uncertainly at Beau. Had he expected the resort owner to be here?

Richter took her hand. "My dear, you look positively radiant. Have you just been getting lots of sun, or—" he paused, looking at Beau and smiling slightly, "—is that glow of yours caused by something else?"

Caitlin cast about for a suitable reply before being rescued by Beau. "What a pleasant surprise, Mr. Richter," he said. "I didn't know you were planning a visit."

"I like to drop in unexpectedly. It keeps the staff on their toes," Richter replied. "But please, don't let me keep you from your dance. Enjoy yourselves. Then maybe you'll join me over at my table." With a wave of his cigar, he indicated a table where the pretty assistant manager sat waiting. She sent Beau and Caitlin a nervous little wave.

There was nothing to do but agree, and the magic had definitely gone out of the dance as Caitlin moved back into Beau's arms. He was stiff and preoccupied, his eyes straying to Richter's table again and again.

"Why don't we just go ahead and join him?" she suggested.

Beau shook his head. "I want a minute to think. I don't know what he's doing here."

"It *is* his resort."

"Yes, but—" The ending swell of music and resulting applause cut off the rest of Beau's reply, and he no longer had any excuse to avoid Richter. "You go on over to his table," he told Caitlin. "I'll let Brenda and Pete know where we are."

An attack of nerves hit Caitlin as she started across the room, and silently she chided herself for foolishness. She was just picking up on Beau's tension. She had to wonder what was causing that. Richter was his client. During the dinner the older man had hosted before they had left for Hilton Head, he and Beau had appeared to be on excellent terms. Why should Beau seem so tense now?

As she approached the table, Richter stood and with an elaborate flourish drew out a chair for her. The assistant manager excused herself, pleading work to do, and Caitlin thought the woman looked decidedly relieved as she made her way toward the door.

Richter chuckled. "The whole staff goes on red alert when they see me coming down the drive. I don't know why. As long as they do their jobs, I'm the best boss in the world."

Caitlin imagined that just doing what this man wanted was a demanding proposition. Wisely, however, she simply nodded and only jumped slightly when he barked out an order. Heads turned at tables across the room as he called, "Waiter! Waiter!"

A young man, red-faced and obviously nervous, came rushing up. "Yes, sir, what can I do for you, sir?"

"The lady here wants a drink," Richter said, his suddenly mild tone belying the urgent summons.

A drink was the last thing Caitlin wanted, but she couldn't refuse when confronted with this young waiter's nervous, perspiring face.

"Make it snappy," Richter instructed him. "And get something for this fella, too." He nodded at Beau, who was slipping into the chair next to Caitlin's. "He likes a real man's drink—a lot of Jack and a little water. Isn't that right?"

"You got it," Beau replied, flashing his usual smooth smile. Gone was the tension Caitlin had sensed in him earlier. Looking at him now, one would never guess that Richter's visit had caught him by surprise.

Their drinks appeared in record time, and Richter cut through the small talk by coming right to the point. "What I want to know is how the work's been going."

"Just great." Beau lounged back in his chair, the picture of unconcern. "In fact, we're going to wrap everything up tomorrow."

Puffing contentedly on his cigar, Richter nodded. "Then I can expect to take a gander at these ads sometime next week?"

"That's right."

"Outstanding." The compliment came like a crash of thunder, followed by a glass-rattling slap on the table. Caitlin jumped, and Richter apologized. "Sorry about that, ma'am. I just get excited when plans start coming together."

"We all do," she assured him. "In fact, I'm really glad this project has gone so well."

Beau's warm green gaze rested on her for a moment. "Caitlin came through like a pro."

"Thanks to you," she murmured, temporarily forgetting that Richter was seated across from them. That special look from Beau made everyone else disappear.

The older man guffawed in obvious delight. "I hate to interrupt this meeting of the mutual admiration society, but I've got some more plans I want to discuss."

Embarrassed at having laid her feelings for Beau out on the table, Caitlin made a move to leave. "If you have business to discuss, I'll just go back to Pete and Brenda."

"But this concerns you," Richter said.

She stared at him in surprise, and a quick glance at Beau's face revealed that he was equally in the dark.

"Exactly what did you have in mind, Mr. Richter?" Beau seemed as relaxed as he had been a few moments earlier, but Caitlin noticed that his eyes narrowed as he took a long sip of his good Tennessee whiskey.

Richter drew out the suspense by sipping his own drink and pausing to take another draw on his cigar. Then he leaned forward, as serious as a head of state discussing nuclear disarmament. "I was sitting in my office the other day," he began dramatically. "And I was trying to think of ways to make the opening of my new resort in Florida special. And I had a brilliant idea." He took a deep breath. "A personal appearance by Scarlett O'Hara."

There was total silence for a moment, and then Beau repeated, "Scarlett O'Hara?"

"Miss Welch, here," Richter said, once again smiling. He winked, too. "Great balls of fire! Won't that be something?"

"Yes, that would be something." Though it was a struggle, Beau summoned an answering grin. Why was it that clients couldn't just leave the advertising and promotional efforts up to him? Why did they always have to come up with some ridiculous idea that only made his life harder?

He had been agreeable to incorporating Richter's *Gone With the Wind* obsession into this ad campaign. In fact, with the help of his agency's creative people, the idea had worked out well. That was because the imagery of the novel and its famous heroine would be used subtly in the finished ads. There would be nothing blatant. The name Scarlett wouldn't even appear in the copy. Carrying it any further was going too far. Richter should stick to building hotels and leave the planning of grand openings to people who knew what they were doing.

"We'll make a big media splash out of it," Richter continued. "The papers will eat it up."

Beau doubted that any papers would give a hoot about the appearance of a Scarlett look-alike at the opening of one more Florida resort. If Vivien Leigh and Clark Gable could be roused from the grave to make an appearance, that *might* capture some attention. This wouldn't. And when the plan caused all the splash of a pebble dropped in the ocean, Richter would blame Beau. End of relationship. End of account. End of six-figure budgets.

But how to tell Richter tactfully that his idea stank? Given the man's volatile nature, that was a tough question. Thank God, Beau didn't have to do it tonight. During the next few months, as they launched this campaign and prepared for the Florida opening, he could *gradually* talk the man out of it. He could *ease* him into—

"But I won't do it."

Caitlin's blunt statement smashed all of Beau's plans for a gentle changing of Richter's mind.

Clutching his cigar like a security blanket, he glared at Caitlin. "What did you say?"

Apparently unaware that she was detonating a bomb, she continued, "I'm honored that you want me to keep on working for your resorts, but I don't think personal appearances are my thing, and—"

"I'd pay you enough to make it your thing," Richter sputtered. He turned to Beau for help. "We can't let that pretty face of hers get away, can we?"

She began to look uncomfortable. "Believe me, I'm flattered, but—"

"Caitlin," Beau cut in, at last finding his voice. "This isn't something we have to decide tonight."

"But I don't want to give Mr. Richter the wrong idea," she insisted. "I wouldn't be opposed to doing more ads, but I'm not comfortable with the idea of—"

"Not comfortable?" The roar was back in Richter's voice. Their waiter, who had been hovering in the background, advanced hesitantly toward their table. Richter brushed him off like an annoying insect. He jabbed the air with his cigar for emphasis. "Let me tell you something, girlie, I've paid you good money to do these ads—"

"Mr. Richter," Beau began.

But Caitlin interrupted him, her voice quiet but insistent. "You've paid me to do this campaign, Mr. Richter. I didn't know I was signing on for more than that." She turned to Beau. "I didn't, did I?"

He let out a breath. "No, you didn't, but—"

"More's the pity." Though he was no longer growling like an injured bear, Richter's disgusted look made it clear he thought Beau had been negligent in not contracting Caitlin's services for life.

Beau tried once again to smooth things over. "Listen, we've got plenty of time to make decisions."

"Which is exactly what I'm going to leave you to do," Caitlin said smoothly, sliding out of her chair. She held her hand out to Richter. "I'm sorry if I've upset your plans."

Ever the gentleman, he stood and enclosed her fingers in his. "We're not through talking about this."

Caitlin bit her lip, and the glance she threw at Beau was imploring. Then she said her goodbyes and left.

Beau stood, silently watching her slender figure weave through the maze of tables to the door.

"I don't like being told no," Richter murmured as he took his seat again.

Beau sat down also and adopted the soothing air that had calmed many clients in the past. He didn't, however, try to reassure the older man. In fact, with Caitlin refusing to go along with his plans, maybe Richter could be convinced to forget the whole thing right now. Beau took a deep breath and began, "I told you from the start that Caitlin wasn't a professional model. We shouldn't really be surprised that she doesn't want to do this—"

"She could be convinced."

"She can be very stubborn. And since there are many other alternatives for making the opening special, I don't think we need to waste our time trying to convince—"

"I'll decide what's a waste of time and what's not," Richter retorted as he lit a fresh cigar. "And I want you to talk her into doing what I want."

"I'm not going to do it." The words came out harsher than Beau intended.

Richter's mouth thinned into an ill-tempered line. "You're not."

"No, I'm not."

"And why, may I ask?"

Beau tried hard to hold his anger in check. Important client or not, he didn't like being treated like a flunky who was supposed to jump when Richter barked out an order. At this point, even if he had thought the man's grand opening scheme was the greatest idea he had ever heard, he would be resisting.

"Well?" Richter prompted.

"Caitlin has her mind made up."

"But you could change it, couldn't you? Even though she's not a model, you convinced her to do these ads." The man paused, his eyes narrowing. "And you're much closer to her now, aren't you?"

"What does that mean?" Beau asked, even though he thought he already knew the answer.

Richter's laugh was low and full of masculine conspiracy. "Come on, son, surely you can convince her to do anything you want. I mean, seeing how you and Miss Welch are so obviously personally involved." The twist he put on that last word made it sound like something dirty.

How Beau resisted throwing his drink in the man's face, he was never sure. He gripped the glass, though, and he kept his voice very low and very steady as he answered. "Whether Caitlin and I are *involved* or not has no bearing on this discussion."

"Oh really?" Incredibly, something akin to a smile flickered across Richter's face. "Then I can assume that you're not going to do what I ask?"

"That's right."

The smile grew even more distinct, and Beau was left with the impression that the man was playing a game. Richter tossed back the last of his drink and for a few moments he regarded Beau in silence. In fact, Beau had started to think he had won this round when Richter spoke. "Let me put it to you this way," he said, still smiling. "Either you convince that little lady of yours to do what I want, or you can forget my business after this campaign is over. How does that sound to you?"

"If that's the way you want it," Beau returned. He forced himself to shrug, as if he weren't bothered in the least by the man's threats. But in his mind a hundred dreams were crashing down. He didn't need the Plantation House Resorts account for just one project. He needed the steady flow of income. So many of his plans hinged on it.

Richter's laughter was soft, and there was a glimmer of admiration in his eyes as he pushed away from the table. "You let me know next week what you're planning to do."

"I can let you know now," Beau said, rising also. "I'm not—"

"You let me know next week," Richter repeated as he turned on his heel.

It wasn't until the older man's absurd white suit had been swallowed up by the crowd that Beau unleashed his temper. Slamming his fist down on the table, he muttered a long and extremely colorful stream of profanity. Instead of satisfaction, all he got for the effort were the annoyed glances of the people occupying the nearby tables. Smothering another curse, he headed outside. He needed to walk off some of his frustration.

The better part of an hour later Caitlin met him at the door of the chalet. She had changed into jeans and T-shirt. With her face pale and eyes wide, she looked more like the woman he had first met than she had in weeks. Beau's heart swelled when he realized how concerned she was. After carrying so many burdens alone for so long, he could get used to knowing that someone cared.

"I'm sorry if I messed things up," she said before he could even get inside.

"It's okay." Beau tossed his navy sport coat over a chair.

"Have I ruined everything?"

He sank down on the couch, suddenly exhausted. "Just come over here and keep me company."

Caitlin needed no further urging to slip into his arms, but she couldn't get her mind off of Richter. "He was awfully angry," she told Beau. "Did you calm him down?"

"No."

She waited for elaboration, but none was forthcoming. With his arm around her, Beau had shut his eyes and leaned his head on the back of the couch. He looked exhausted, but she couldn't seem to leave the situation alone. "You do understand why I don't want to make that stupid appearance, don't you? Posing for an ad is one thing, but I don't want to start running around from resort to resort, pretending to be Scarlett O'Hara."

He nodded.

"And you're not angry?"

His sigh seemed to come from somewhere deep inside of him. But he opened his eyes, and his voice was far from angry. "Of course not."

"So what will you do?"

Beau's hesitation was slight, as was the frown that flickered across his face. "I'll work something out." His frown turned quickly to a mischievous grin. "Personally, I think Richter should forget the resort business and start a fried-chicken empire. He already has the wardrobe for it. All he needs is the secret recipe of some little white-haired lady in Georgia. Maybe they could do the television commercials together. He could stand there in his white suit, and she could say, 'Where's the chicken?' What do you think? Has it been done to death?"

In just minutes he had Caitlin laughing, and it wasn't until the next day that she realized how neatly he had distracted her from questions about Richter. Just as neatly, he sidestepped her further attempts at discussing the matter. Caitlin knew something was on Beau's mind, however, and she'd lay odds that it was Richter. But that afternoon, as they headed north toward Chattanooga, she gave up trying to get Beau to talk about it. As usual, he turned her every question into one of his own.

It bothered her more and more that he never really opened up to her. Beau was quick to retreat behind his ready smile and quick wit, to share a joke or laugh. But that was all he shared. Aside from a few details about his childhood, she knew little about him. Of course that wasn't entirely true. She knew he was intelligent and charming, respected by those who worked for him, adept at turning most situations to his advantage. She also knew the secrets that only a lover can know, knowledge shared in sighs and whispers. But there had to be more. She wanted to know the man behind his handsome, smiling facade. She wanted to look inside his heart.

While the miles slipped past outside the car window, the doubts Caitlin had been avoiding began to eat away at her. Perhaps all that lay between her and Beau was surface flash. Unlike her, perhaps he didn't want to know the person she was inside. Maybe this was nothing more than a superficial affair for him.

But if that were the truth, why was she on her way to meet his parents?

Remembering their destination, her jumbled thoughts settled down. Seeing Beau with his family would probably provide her with answers for many of her questions about him. She already knew his relationship with his parents wasn't close. But that relationship had shaped the man that he was, the man that she loved. She could learn a great deal about him this weekend.

She was quickly confronted with her first lesson. It came from the house where his parents lived.

Caitlin had known Beau's family was wealthy, but she hadn't expected their time-mellowed brick-and-stone mansion. The house and surrounding grounds spoke of something more than mere wealth. The scent of money hung on the air, as undiluted as the fragrance of newly mown grass on the afternoon breeze. She should have expected this, of course, as soon as Beau had explained where his parents lived. Lookout Mountain, standing guard as it did over the city of Chattanooga, had long been the home of some of the South's wealthiest, most influential people. Statesmen, diplomats, tycoons—all had and did call this their home. It was appropriate that the handsome, assured man by her side could do the same.

But if he belonged here, why had he been borrowing the apartment next to hers? And he did belong here, as surely as Caitlin belonged in her neighborhood of struggling educators and impoverished college students.

She was silent as they started down the sidewalk; and he must have sensed her unease, for he squeezed her hand. "The old homestead is a bit overwhelming, isn't it?"

"Maybe a little."

He paused on the shallow front steps and surveyed the front of the house, grinning. "Would you believe that in one summer I broke every ground floor window here on the front?"

Imagining shenanigans of that nature from him wasn't hard. "How?" she asked, smiling.

"Baseball." He turned back to the immaculate front yard. "For some reason, my friends and I decided this was the perfect place to practice."

"And your parents kept letting you, even after you broke all the windows?"

His smile was wicked. "The trick was waiting until Mother left for the garden club or lunch with her friends or an appointment with her hairdresser. By the time the housekeeper got wind of what was happening, the game would be well underway."

"Sounds to me as if you were deliberately provoking your parents."

Squeezing her hand again, he laughed. "How very perceptive of you, Miss Welch. Of course I was provoking my parents. There was nothing I liked doing more."

A vague suspicion nibbled at the back of Caitlin's mind. "Is that what you still like to do?"

Beau shook his head. "I gave that up a couple of years ago, about the time I stopped bringing wild women up here to meet them."

"Wild women?"

"Highly inappropriate creatures on whom my mother could practice her ice-queen act."

His explanation was hardly reassuring. Caitlin swallowed and studied the front door with growing trepidation. "Is that how she's going to treat me?"

"Of course not. I told—" His words were interrupted by the opening of the door.

The woman who stood there was undoubtedly his mother, but she didn't appear icy at all. Her warm gold hair was streaked with silver. Her eyes were a vibrant blue. Her movements were those of a person who was full of energy, the same sort of energy habitually radiated by her son. And clearly, she was happy to see him.

"Mother," Beau said, stepping forward. The kiss he pressed on her cheek was lacking in warmth, and some of the pleasure left her expression. She brightened visibly, however, when Beau introduced Caitlin.

"We're so glad you could come." The genuine pleasure in her eyes robbed the words of their formality. Her gaze skimmed Caitlin from head to toe and back again, but her smile remained in place.

Realizing that she had been holding her breath, Caitlin let it out. "I'm glad to be here," she murmured politely.

"Where's Dad?" Beau asked, tossing the car keys on a table beside the door.

"Out by the pool," his mother answered. "We'll go out there now and have something cool to drink. Just leave your bags till later."

Just like Dorothy on her way to meet the great and powerful wizard, Caitlin thought as their footsteps echoed down a long central foyer. Doors on the right and left revealed beautifully decorated rooms. Living room. Library. Dining room. Den. She smoothed a damp palm down one thigh, suddenly wishing she had worn something a little more stylish than the khaki slacks and red blouse that had looked so smart and so crisp this morning. In this house beside Beau's mother, she felt like the gauche and unattractive person she had been for most of her life.

The pool was a large oval beyond a rear veranda. Colorful striped umbrellas shaded a number of tables, and a matching awning sheltered the poolside cabana. A man was stretched out in one of the lounge chairs grouped beside this structure. He got slowly to his feet as they approached.

So this is Beau's father, Caitlin thought. He was just as she had imagined he would be. As tall as Beau. Almost as trim. With shoulders he held straight and proud. Caitlin allowed herself a moment's pity for the lawyers and criminals who had probably faced this handsome attorney. His confident bearing alone would make him a formidable opponent. He certainly didn't look like a sick man. Although he was a little pale, she decided as Beau performed the introductions, and there was a fatigued look about his green eyes.

Beau's mother, who had asked Caitlin to call her Martha, left them alone while she went inside to get some lemonade. The two men studied each other in silence.

"So what's this I hear about your overdoing it?" Beau finally asked his father.

"A bunch of nonsense," came the reply. But Caitlin couldn't help noticing the long sigh he breathed when he once again stretched out in the lounge chair.

Beau appeared to notice it, also, for a frown furrowed the skin between his eyebrows. "It doesn't look like nonsense to me."

His father sighed again, this time in annoyance. "It *is* nonsense. A little rest, and I'll be just fine. Your mother shouldn't have called and bothered you. I understand you were busy with a project for an important client." He sat up a little straighter, voice quickening with interest. "Anyone I know?"

"I doubt it." Beau's answer was cryptic, bordering on rude. Was it Caitlin's imagination or did his father almost wince at the tone? She waited for Beau to fill in the awkward pause that followed, but he said nothing.

Feeling she had to bridge the gap, she asked about the age and construction of the house. It turned out that she and Mr. Collins—Perry, he insisted—shared an interest in history, and by the time Martha arrived with a tray of lemonade, they were involved in a lively discussion of the role Lookout Mountain had played in the Civil War.

"If the Confederates hadn't held the mountain as long as they did, the Yankees would have been in Atlanta long before Sherman's march," Perry concluded. Then he chuckled. "Since then, of course, Yankees have been making regular invasions of that city."

"Now, Perry," Martha cautioned. "You shouldn't speak so harshly of the North. The war was over more than a hundred years ago. And for all you know, Caitlin's family fought for the other side."

"Actually, my ancestors are from Kentucky," Caitlin explained. "One great-great-grandfather fought for the North. His brother went for the South, and supposedly most of the ancestors on my mother's side just lit out for California to avoid the whole bloomin' mess."

"And perhaps they were the smartest of all," Beau commented amid the general laughter.

"Maybe," she agreed. "The only problem is that, by leaving, they scattered the family. I probably have relatives in every part of the country, but I don't know any of them. I've always regretted knowing so little about them."

"Oh, you shouldn't regret it," Beau drawled in a deceptively mild tone. "Sometimes knowing every accomplishment of your ancestors can be rather boring, especially when you're expected to follow in their footsteps."

While a sudden silence greeted his observation, he merely drained the last of his lemonade. His mother studied the diamonds in her wedding band with rapt attention. His father shifted his gaze to stare at a point somewhere beyond them all, frowning.

Lesson number two, Caitlin thought, this family is divided by some bitter wounds. Wounds Beau seemed to want to deepen.

"I'm going to go and get our bags," he muttered, pushing himself out of his chair.

Caitlin was left to try and make conversation. His parents quickly recovered their poise, but she grew more uncomfortable with each passing moment.

*I don't belong here,* she told herself. Not in this elegant, antique-filled house. Not with this troubled family. Why had Beau brought her here, anyway?

Her feelings of unease built as the afternoon faded to evening, even though Perry and Martha tried their best to make Caitlin feel welcome. Dinner was a casual affair, with just the four of them, but the atmosphere was strained and uncomfortable. Afterward, some friends of Beau's parents dropped by to see how Perry was feeling.

The visiting couple, whom Martha said were lifelong friends and neighbors, greeted Beau with affection and regarded Caitlin with open curiosity. Certainly Martha's introduction did little to appease their questions. "This is Caitlin Welch," she said. "Caitlin is Beau's—umm—Beau's friend."

The stumble was slight enough to have gone unnoticed. But Caitlin thought it most appropriate. For who was she, anyway? Beau's employee? His lover? All she knew was that for a month she had been acting like someone totally unlike herself. Sooner or later, she was going to have to go back to the regular Caitlin. Oh, that didn't mean she had to go back to looking plain, but her life was hardly glamorous. It certainly wasn't the sort of life that prepared a girl for mansions and the subtle but sharp infighting of wealthy families.

Finally, she pleaded an all-too-real headache and retreated to the comfortable peach-and-gray bedroom she had been given. Beau had placed his own bags in the room across the hall, and she could only suppose he was going to honor his mother's implied assumption that they wouldn't be sharing a room. But she lay awake for a long time, hoping he would come in and enclose her in his strong, familiar arms.

Beau figured his family had been too much for Caitlin, and she needed time alone. Long after his parents' friends left, he sat on the back veranda, thinking about what had transpired last night with Richter. Little else had been on his mind all afternoon, and it had put him in a foul mood, so foul he had even tried to pick a fight with his parents. That hadn't been his intention. He wanted this visit to be pleasant, wanted them to like Caitlin. Everything was going well on that point, as he had known it would. Caitlin was perfect. A little nervous, very respectful, making intelligent conversation, looking crisp and polished. He could tell his parents were impressed.

His world would be perfect if only Richter would cooperate. Perhaps he could do as the man wanted and convince Caitlin....

No! Beau resisted the very thought. He wasn't going to ask her. First of all, he still thought the idea was stupid. But secondly, and much more importantly, he wouldn't use their personal relationship for business purposes. He would find another solution to his problem. Right now he was going to go to bed and put it all out of his mind. Maybe things would look better in the morning.

He was passing through the foyer toward the back stairs when his father called out to him. A perverse demon, born of habit, tempted Beau to pretend he didn't hear. But chiding himself silently for his childishness, he went into the family room.

Soft music was playing on the stereo, and both of his parents were settled into chairs, looking comfortable. His father's pipe scented the air. His mother had even kicked off her shoes. Beau raised an eyebrow at that. She so seldom had even a wrinkle in her skirt.

"You're both up late," he murmured as he sprawled on the sofa. "Shouldn't you be getting some rest, sir?"

"All I've done for the past few days is rest," his father complained.

His mother chuckled. "And that's all you should be doing."

"While those dunderheads at the office foul up everything."

"If they're dunderheads, you shouldn't have hired them," she admonished gently and slid her feet into her shoes. She stood. "I'm going up to bed. Beau, you make sure your father comes up soon." Her hand lingered on her husband's shoulder as she started to leave. Briefly, he covered her fingers with his own.

Despite everything, she's always loved him, Beau thought. *Everything* included long hours, canceled vacations and—Beau suspected—an affair or two. During the summer he had worked at his father's office, there had been an attractive young lawyer with whom Perry Collins had spent more than the usual amount of time. And while he had been home one

Christmas break, he had seen his father having a drink with a sexy neighbor, a woman who later tried to make a move on Beau at a holiday party. Surely his mother knew about these indiscretions. Nothing remained a secret for long in their closed little social circle. Most likely some of Martha's so-called friends had tried their luck with her rich and handsome husband.

Yet she still loved him. Or at least she seemed to. That, like so much of their lives, might be just a ceremony, another attempt to keep up the appearances they valued so highly.

"Beau?"

He glanced up, realizing that his mother was speaking to him from the doorway. "Yes?"

Her voice was soft. "We like Caitlin," she said. "She's a lovely, intelligent girl. I hope you can both stay for a few days, so I can get to know her better."

Beau merely nodded. Even though he had known his parents would like Caitlin, he hadn't expected them to say so in such a forthright matter.

"I'd like to see you settled down with someone like her," Martha continued. "Someone who could make you happy."

Happy. The word lingered even after the sound of his mother's footsteps had disappeared up the back staircase. It wasn't what Beau would have expected to hear. He would have expected his mother to say Caitlin would make him a good partner or a gracious hostess. When had his happiness become a concern of theirs?

His father, too, was nodding. "She is a lovely girl."

Before pausing to think, Beau said, "I love her." It was the first time he had said those words aloud, and they suddenly seemed an inadequate description of his feelings for Caitlin. "Very much," he added, and chanced a look at his father's face. The man had never been fond of emotional displays.

But Perry merely nodded again. "I guess you're thinking of marriage."

"Eventually," Beau said evasively. "Caitlin and I haven't known each other that long."

Now his father looked surprised. "I would think that a man your age, with a successful business and a solid future wouldn't need to think very long about getting married and starting a family."

For a moment Beau studied his father's face, hoping to find a clue to the hidden meaning behind those words. Was he, in his usual subtle way, trying to get Beau to admit his business troubles? His expression gave nothing away, and Beau was left wondering if the man's interest could be taken at face value. The last time he had visited, his father had also been pleasant. Could it be he was mellowing? That was hard for Beau to believe. For too long he and his father had been locked in a struggle of wills. For too many years he had felt as if the man was just waiting for him to stumble.

Every time he had faltered, his father had been waiting to rub salt into the wound. Vividly, Beau could remember what had happened following the last football game of his college career. His father had been in the stands for the first time that year, and as bad luck would have it, Beau had been injured during a punt return in the fourth quarter. The damage to his knee had been severe enough to put him out for the rest of the year. The disappointing end to his football career was bad enough, but even worse had been his father's reaction.

"Didn't I tell you," he had muttered. "Didn't I say this football nonsense would get you nowhere?" The fact that his son had loved that *nonsense* had meant very little to him. He had just wanted to have the last word, to be right.

Since then, Beau had asked his father for only one thing—the money to start his agency. When that had been denied, Beau had been more determined than ever to make sure his father wasn't right about everything. No matter what troubles he had, with his parents he pretended as if everything in his world was just fine.

In a sense, he was perhaps no better than his parents. For he played their game of pretense and appearances very well.

Now he summoned a smile and an explanation. "The agency is going terrific, Father. But it's still going to be a while before I ask Caitlin to marry me. We need some time to get used to each other."

"Well, you know best," Perry returned. An unexpected smile softened his normally stern features. "Although, I have to tell you that your mother and I wouldn't be opposed to a couple of grandchildren." He hesitated then, and his voice roughened, his eyes strayed from Beau's. "And I can promise you that we won't preach to them about the accomplishments of their ancestors."

The words were an echo of what Beau had said earlier. He regretted letting that slip. "That remark was uncalled for," he said automatically, knowing the apology was expected.

"Maybe not."

Surprised into speechlessness, Beau stared hard at his father.

"Maybe your mother and I made a lot of mistakes," Perry murmured, his voice still rough. "From the beginning you were a person who didn't fit the molds. You never did anything on the schedule those damned baby books of your mother's laid out." He laughed then and finally looked at Beau again. "I don't know why we kept trying to change you, kept trying to raise you in exactly the way we had been raised."

"Is that what you were trying to do?"

"Yes. And we were raised to think that family tradition and holding a certain place in society was the most important thing in the world."

"You tried pretty hard to pound that into me." Those lectures on family were still vivid in Beau's mind. Maybe if they hadn't tried so hard... He shook his head. "All you did was make me angry," he muttered.

"Yes, we did," his father agreed. "And that was our mistake, the one we live with." He sighed, and the sound was sad.

Beau could think of nothing to say. And so they sat together, father and son, listening to the clock in the foyer strike twelve times. His father went to bed soon after. And still Beau lingered. The old house sighed and creaked, providing a suitable background for his thoughts.

On the one hand, it amazed him that his father had admitted to making a mistake. On the other, he was suspicious. Why was his father reaching out to him at long last? Maybe his collapse had given him a taste of his own mortality. Maybe he thought he should put his house in order before it was too late.

But a few words couldn't erase a lifetime of rejection and resentment. A few words couldn't change how Beau felt. It would take more than a softly spoken wish for grandchildren to make him really believe his father had changed.

"We'll see," Beau told himself. And for the briefest of moments he allowed himself to hope and to grin at the improbable thought of his stern, uncompromising father bouncing a baby on his knee.

## *Chapter Ten*

Something tickled Caitlin's nose, rousing her from sleep. A pesky fly, she thought groggily, swatting the insect away before rolling onto her stomach.

"Wake up, beautiful."

She opened one eye. Flies didn't talk. She turned over and found Beau seated on the edge of her bed, holding a steaming mug of coffee and one perfect, yellow rose.

"I come bearing gifts." He smiled and set the mug on the bedside table. "But I think what you really need is a kiss."

"You're right." She sat up and melted into his arms, translating all of last night's lonely misery into the intensity of her kiss.

Finally, Beau drew away. "Wow. Maybe I should have come in here earlier."

"I missed you last night," Caitlin whispered. The sophisticated lovers he was no doubt used to might never have admitted such a thing, but at this moment she didn't care. It had taken only a few days to get used to sleeping with Beau. "Where were you?"

He dropped another kiss on her mouth. "Across the hall, surrounded by football trophies and shelves full of Hardy Boys mysteries."

Smiling in understanding, she nodded. "It's Nancy Drew in my old room at home."

"I always thought Joe and Frank Hardy should have teamed up with Nancy and a couple of her friends. It would have been much more interesting if they had done some of this." Beau kissed her again, harder this time.

"I think that would have gotten them all into a lot of trouble," Caitlin murmured against his lips.

"You call this trouble?" His laugh was low and sexy. "I'll show you trouble." Through the satiny material of her gown, his fingers teased the budding peak of her breast.

Closing her eyes, Caitlin arched her neck backward. "Nancy would have never allowed this."

"She never was any fun," Beau growled against the skin of her throat. "Not like you." But his hands fell away from her.

"What's wrong? Are you having second thoughts about ravishing me in your parent's house?"

"I'd be willing to ravish you anywhere," he answered and paused to draw his hand through her tumbled hair, seemingly fascinated with the way it fell to her shoulders. "But unfortunately, I need to check in at the Chattanooga office."

A feeling close to panic gripped Caitlin. "Can I go with you?"

"What's wrong?" he asked, grinning. "Afraid to stay in this mausoleum with my parents?"

"No, of course not," Caitlin lied. "I'd just like to meet everyone at the agency. Molly told me about everyone—"

"Some other time, okay?" Beau interrupted, and a shadow seemed to darken his eyes. "I've got a lot of stuff to do this morning. Besides," he said when she started to protest again. "My parents really like you."

"They said so?"

He nodded and kissed her again. "You know what? I think you are the only thing I've ever done that they've approved of without reservation."

Being referred to as a "thing" wasn't entirely reassuring, but Beau gave her no time to protest. Instead, he stood and dropped the yellow rose into her lap.

"My cousin Melissa is going to come up this afternoon," he said. "She should keep you from being bored to death by Mother and Father."

Caitlin summoned a smile of agreement. There was little else she could do. Beau would think she was silly if she protested any further. Even though he wasn't close to his parents, it was obviously important to him that they like her. What that said about his feelings for her she wasn't sure. But she badly wanted to please him.

So she smiled as he left her room. Then she slipped from her bed, and from the window overlooking the front yard, she watched his car disappear down the drive. It was some moments before she realized that in her clutching hand she had crushed the delicate petals of the rose. Their scent drifted upward, mocking the senseless taste of foreboding that rose in her mouth.

She tried hard to shake off that feeling. There was really nothing to fear in the quietly elegant surroundings of Beau's parents' home. Nor was there anything frightening about the smiles of those two attractive people. Quite the contrary, they seemed to want to put Caitlin at ease. Over a late breakfast served on the veranda, they asked subtle, tactful questions that encouraged her to tell them about her education, her work and her family.

She told them about Julie, half expecting their faces to settle into the polite mask of distaste so many people felt for the mentally handicapped. But instead, they made only intelligent, informed observations and expressed an admiration for Caitlin's decision to work with children who shared her sister's handicap.

Gradually, Caitlin relaxed, and she began to wonder why Beau couldn't get along with these charming people. As the day wore on, she started to think the problems might be of Beau's own making. It was a disloyal thought, however, and she tried hard to shake it.

Beau's cousin, Melissa, made her appearance in midafternoon. Though she was friendly and unaffected as they sat around one of the tables beside the pool, she looked to be the sort of woman who had always made Caitlin feel tall and gawky and awkward. No more than five foot four, with blond hair and blue eyes, she bore a striking resemblance to her Aunt Martha. They had the same perfect, porcelain complexion and delicately arched eyebrows. Both of them carried themselves with an innate confidence.

The illusion of perfection, however, was dispelled by Melissa's lack of artifice. She wore neither make-up nor jewelry other than her engagement ring and wedding band. The bathing suit revealed under her shorts was a utilitarian black maillot that sported a small hole on one side.

"Would you look at that?" she said. "No telling how old this suit is. It's been so long since I've been swimming that I haven't bothered to buy a new one."

"You know you're welcome to come up here any time," Martha admonished.

"I know," Melissa replied. "But I just don't have time."

"Can't that restaurant run itself without you?" Beau's father asked.

"Oh, and listen to the workaholic talking," Martha retorted.

They all laughed at his rueful smile, yet Caitlin thought Melissa studied Beau's parents with something akin to amazement. That suspicion was confirmed later, when Martha and Perry moved inside out of the heat, leaving the two younger women alone beside the pool.

"Boy, you must have worked a miracle on them," Melissa said, amazement clearly apparent as she nodded in the direction of the house.

Pausing in the process of slathering on suntan oil, Caitlin frowned, not knowing how to interpret the remark.

Melissa chuckled and rummaged in her dilapidated beach bag. "I mean, they're acting so nice. It's such a switch for them."

"What do you mean?"

"To the best of my memory, the only other time I've seen Uncle Perry smile was on the night my father was first elected to Congress." She grinned. "And lord knows, Aunt Martha hasn't treated me this well since before Father had to resign. She set such stock on having a brother in the national limelight."

Until this moment, Caitlin had forgotten that Melissa's father was Malcolm Chambers, an ex-congressman. A scandal had forced the man from office several years ago. Beau had told Caitlin that the experience had been hard on Melissa's entire family. Her parents had divorced, her younger brother had bounced from one mess to the other, and Melissa had floundered for personal direction. Only with the opening of her restaurant and her marriage to her business partner, Hunt Kirkland, had she set her life on an even keel. Her brother was following suit.

Now, watching Melissa twist her hair up in an untidy ponytail, it was hard for Caitlin to imagine that the pretty blonde had ever had a care in the world. Her smile was open and honest, and she was easy to talk with.

"Beau's parents have been very nice ever since I got here," Caitlin said. "I don't think it's anything I've done."

"Beau told me that they liked you," Melissa murmured, accepting the bottle of oil from Caitlin.

"You've talked to Beau today?"

"He came by the restaurant for a free lunch. Typical of him, isn't it?" she explained, laughing. "Beau said his parents might be mellowing, but I didn't believe him. I guess maybe he was right."

"Were they so hard on him before?" Caitlin thought someone else's perspective might reveal a story different from Beau's.

Melissa's answer was a rather indelicate snort. "Hard isn't the exact description I would use. More like impossible. He never did anything well enough to please them."

Caitlin was silent, gazing at the big house for a moment. "That seems so ridiculous. I mean, Beau is so perfect. He's intelligent, handsome, successful..." Too late she realized all she was revealing about her feelings for him.

But in Melissa's smile she saw nothing but pleasure. "You're talking like a woman in love," she said.

Flushing, Caitlin turned away.

"Hey, I think it's great." Melissa laughed. "When Beau told me he had finally brought the right sort of woman home, I was afraid you'd be some stuffy, boring paragon."

Caitlin laughed at the description. "I was pretty stuffy before I met Beau." The story of her transformation into a model spilled out, along with all of her doubts. "I don't know," she said at last, drawing an unsteady breath. "Sometimes I think I've changed too much. I get worried that it's only my looks that attract Beau."

Melissa cocked her head to the side, her expression thoughtful. "I won't lie to you," she said at last. "Beau has always liked pretty women. But none of them ever held his attention for long. There has to be something going on behind the pretty face."

Despite the heat of the afternoon, Caitlin shivered. She didn't know that Beau knew or cared what went on in her head. Not that he was thoughtless or condescending, but their whole relationship had been such a whirlwind affair. She knit her brow, trying to remember what they had ever talked about. Her family. Her work. Tom. But in depth? Thinking back over the last passion-clouded week, it was hard to remember exactly what she had told him about herself. And certainly they had talked very little about him. Aside from making sure she achieved the right look for the ads, desire had seemed to be the subject most on his mind during the last week.

"I think Beau's got everything he could possibly want in you," Melissa said soberly, interrupting Caitlin's introspection. "Hunt told me you were brilliant—"

"Hunt said that about me?" Coming from her handsome, levelheaded landlord, Caitlin thought the compliment rather extravagant.

But Melissa nodded. "He really admires what you do at the school."

"He's made some generous contributions," Caitlin said. "They can always find teachers, but without people like him, there would be no school."

A gentle smile touched Melissa's lips. "He's pretty terrific," she murmured, the love shining in her eyes. "I hope you and Beau find what Hunt and I have, Caitlin. Beau's the best. I want what's right for him. Once he gets all his business problems worked out, I know that absolutely everything will work out between you two, also."

Caitlin frowned. "Business problems?"

"You know," Melissa said, waving a hand. "All this mess with that Richter character. If Beau didn't need that account so badly, it wouldn't matter so much that the man has pulled his business. I don't know exactly what happened between them. . . ."

Her voice faded as a sick feeling settled in Caitlin's stomach. *So I did mess everything up,* she thought. Why hadn't Beau told her? She tried to concentrate on what Melissa was saying.

"Of course, Beau thinks he can smooth things over with Richter."

Caitlin nodded automatically. Of course Beau could smooth things out. He could talk anybody into anything. Couldn't he? A pinprick of doubt nudged her confidence aside, spurred by the memory of Beau's tension when Richter had appeared at the resort. She had never seen Beau nervous before. But Richter was just an account, wasn't he? It wasn't life or death.

Melissa's words told a different story. "It's been one thing after another for Beau this year." Mutely, Caitlin listened as Beau's cousin chronicled the last troubled year in the life of Beau's agency. The explanation went right along with the tough breaks Molly had once hinted at when talking about the agency. The Richter account was a do-or-die business proposition. Hunt and Melissa had already lent a financial hand, help that Beau had insisted be regarded as an investment. He refused any further help. He needed business, not another loan.

Finally, Melissa broke off, shaking her head. "I don't know why I'm rattling on like this. You probably know better than anyone how much Beau needs Richter's account." She stopped, studying Caitlin in silence. "You do know, don't you?"

Caitlin shook her head.

"Damn," Melissa muttered, biting her lip. "I just thought Beau would have shared his troubles with you."

"Yes, one would have thought that, wouldn't one?" Caitlin's tone was brittle.

"Now, Caitlin," Melissa began. "Beau is very private. He's always kept his problems to himself."

"He told you, didn't he?"

"But he's always told me things, the same as I've confided in him." Melissa put a hand on Caitlin's arm, obviously troubled. "The older generation in our family hasn't always been willing to listen."

Caitlin was silent.

Melissa attempted to reassure her. "Beau is so distracted and worried right now that he probably thinks he *has* told you."

That seemed unlikely, but rather than upset Melissa further, Caitlin murmured agreement and changed the subject by suggesting a swim. Stroking through the cool water, she tried to push her questions aside. But they grew more insistent.

Why hadn't Beau told her that Richter was pulling his business? If the issue of her doing that stupid publicity-stunt appearance had caused the rift, then she could easily mend it. Why hadn't Beau just asked her to do it? A simple, straightforward question would have solved it.

Simple. Straightforward. Did those words really apply to Beau? She had to admit they didn't. He was too complicated an individual for words like that to fit. Not a dishonest person, certainly. But she had decided long ago that he was a man with many sides, and one of those sides was skilled in making people do exactly what he wanted. Moreover, he could convince people that doing what *he* wanted was *their own* idea. Why, she had seen him talk Pete and Brenda and Molly into a host of things. He had charmed cooperation out of clerks, drivers, waiters. He had manipulated her into...

Manipulated? Caitlin was shocked by her own description. Beau hadn't manipulated her. Oh, he had talked her into doing the ads. But that was business. He hadn't manipulated her in any personal way.

*Had he?*

The question loomed larger and grew uglier as she waited for Beau to come home. He appeared late in the day with Hunt in tow. Seeing Hunt and Melissa together did little for Caitlin's frame of mind. They were so openly, honestly in love, so in tune that each could complete the other's sentences. Perhaps it was unfair to compare them to herself and Beau. After all, Hunt and Melissa had been together for a year. She had barely known Beau a month.

And that was the most disturbing part of all her questions, she decided. She hadn't known Beau long enough to know what he was capable of doing.

Valiantly, she tried to put her worries aside, to hold on to the fact that she loved him. She tried to reassure herself about his intentions. He was her lover because he desired her. He had brought her here to meet his family because she was important to him, important in a way that had nothing to do with business. That was what she hoped, anyway.

At Martha's insistence, Hunt and Melissa stayed for dinner. Beau was in top form, regaling everyone with outrageous stories. Unlike the night before, he didn't bait his parents with sarcasm. The evening was so relaxed and enjoyable that it was late when Hunt and

Melissa stood at the front door, saying their goodbyes.

"I hope to see you again, very soon," Melissa murmured, giving Caitlin a little hug.

"Same here," Hunt said.

To Caitlin's surprise, Martha stepped forward and slipped an arm around her waist. "Don't you two worry. I'm going to make sure Beau doesn't let this pretty face get away."

*Pretty face.*

The words chased around and around in Caitlin's head before clicking into place. For weeks now, her face had been everyone's concern. Ever since that night Beau had crashed into her apartment—

". . . quite a face," he had said that night.

"I always said you had a pretty face," her mother had said a few days later.

"We can't let this pretty face of hers get away, can we?" Richter had asked Beau.

*Pretty face.*

*Her pretty face.*

My God. With growing horror, Caitlin realized a pretty face was all she had become.

*A pretty face was all she was to Beau.*

Mechanically, she said her last goodbye to Hunt and Melissa and watched Beau walk out to the car with them. She smiled at his parents and made an excuse about leaving something on the back veranda. Heart pounding, she hurried through the house. Once outside, she slumped against the cool stone of the house and drew the hot July air into her lungs with big, gasping breaths.

How ironic it was. Caitlin Welch, perennial ugly duckling, had become a victimized swan. Heavens, how she had preened for Beau. One kiss from him, and she had gone scampering for fine new feathers, eager to remake herself into the person she imagined he wanted her to be.

Quite clearly, she could remember that morning in New Orleans after she and Beau had made love for the first time. Even then, she had known that people like herself weren't supposed to feel that good. Nice little ordinary girls weren't supposed to feel so special. She had been playing a role, acting out a fantasy. Her dream. Beau's. Oh, she had become a person he could desire, all right. A person he could manipulate. Once before she had wondered if he might be using her. Why, oh why hadn't she trusted her own inclinations then?

"Caitlin?" Beau came out of the shadows at the edge of the veranda. "What are you doing out here?"

"Clearing my head," she whispered. "Something I should have done weeks ago."

He came closer, until his handsome features were touched by the light streaming from the family-room windows. He was frowning. "What do you mean?"

She laughed, and the sound fell between them like shards of broken glass. "This has been quite a few weeks we've had, hasn't it?"

Still frowning, he nodded. "You could say that, but—"

"You've had yourself quite a time."

He stepped forward, an arm outstretched. "Caitlin, I don't—"

"Please," she murmured, flinching away. "Don't touch me."

"What in God's name is wrong?"

She didn't waste any time on niceties. "You've been using me."

His lips repeated the words, silently, the way a game-show contestant repeats a question for which he has no answer.

"You could have just asked me to do that appearance for Richter," she said bitterly. "I would have done almost anything you asked—"

"But I don't want—"

"You didn't have to bring me here to meet your parents or pretend that I was something special before you asked me. I would have done it anyway, just because you asked."

"But you are special. That is why I brought you here," he protested. "I wanted my parents to meet you."

"And what does that get you?"

A muscle beside his mouth twitched. "Get me?"

Caitlin clenched her hands, barely aware of the nails that dug into her palms. "You might as well be honest, you know. The jig is up. I've figured it all out. You flirted with me to keep me happy and agreeable during the shoot."

"That's not true—"

Tears stung her eyes. "But you didn't really have to sleep with me, you know. I would have been content with a few kisses—"

His hands closed on her shoulders, and struggle though she did, he held her steady. "What's wrong with you? Making love—"

"Don't call it that." Her voice rose on a hysterical note. "You know what it's really called. You f—"

"Don't!" he shouted and gave her a little shake. "Don't say that, Caitlin. I don't know where you've gotten these stupid ideas."

"Stupid?" She laughed again and succeeded in breaking free of his hands. She backed away from him. "That was your mistake, because I'm not stupid. I've got something behind this *pretty, pretty face.*" She spat the last words at him.

He came forward, hands held out in an imploring gesture. "You're not making any sense."

"That's all I am to you. A face." She swept her hair back. "I was the face you needed to get Richter's account. I'm the face you need to keep it. That's the only value I have for you." Her hair fell forward, and she clenched her eyes shut. "And when you got what you wanted from me I would have been gone. You didn't think I was smart enough to figure that out, did you?"

He grabbed her arm. "Look at me," he shouted until she had no choice but to open her eyes. "I'm not using you. I told Richter to go to hell. I love you."

How coincidental that he had never told her this before, Caitlin thought sarcastically. "Oh, tell me another one."

"I do love you."

Jerking away from him again, she started toward the door to the family room. "If you're in love it's with a face, an image that isn't even real."

"That's not true—"

"I never knew I was such a good actress," she said, fumbling for the doorknob. "But I became everything you wanted. Just the right mixture. Devil enough to take to bed. Angel enough to bring home to Mom and Dad."

Saint and sinner, Beau thought. Yes, that was what he had seen in those first photographs of her. God, but that seemed like such a long time ago. The woman in front of him was now much more than just a face he needed for an ad campaign. Perhaps she had always been more than that. Perhaps he had started loving her from the first, when she had faced him with a gun clutched in a shaking hand. Brave but vulnerable. Strong but unquestionably feminine. She was everything he had ever wanted, and she couldn't just walk out of his life.

Abandoning her attempts to get the door to the family room open, Caitlin wheeled around to face him. "How convenient for you that I was the sort of girl Mom and Dad could like. Having pleased them at last, what did you have in mind next? What did you want from *them*?"

With her taunting words, something in Beau's gaze seemed to splinter. Once more, he seized her shoulders, but this time he didn't shout. He didn't shake her. He just stared down into her tear-streaked face.

"I'm not asking my parents for anything." His voice was clear and distinct and utterly cold. "They've never helped me when I've really needed it. And they'd be damn happy to see me lose my business. Father always said I would."

"Poor little rich boy rebel," Caitlin muttered sarcastically.

"Yeah, that's me." His lips twisted into the bitterest of smiles. "Such a disappointment. Again."

With those words Caitlin found she at last had her wish. She was looking straight into the heart of the man she had yearned to know. Gone was the laughter, the quick sidestepping wit, the perfect person she had tried to describe to her mother. All his vulnerabilities, his fears of failure were exposed. Standing before her was just the man, with the accompanying doubts and insecurities of any mortal.

And in that moment she discovered she loved the man more than she had ever loved the ideal.

"Son." The low, strangled word brought her head snapping around. Beau's father stood in the doorway to the family room. There was just enough light for her to see the horror-stricken look on his face.

Beau stiffened and released her, and it seemed to Caitlin that he cloaked himself in some invisible armor.

"Never a disappointment," his father choked out. "A challenge to understand, yes. Different from me. But never a disappointment."

"Father—" Beau began in a voice that shook with emotion.

Caitlin never heard the rest of what he said. She fled. In her room, she grabbed her purse. She left her clothes. Most of them belonged to another person, anyway. The keys to Beau's rental car were on the table next to the front door, exactly where she had seen him toss them the day before. She grabbed them and left, not once looking back at the big, shadowed house.

It was only two hours later, safe in her mother's house in Knoxville, that she allowed herself to cry.

## *Chapter Eleven*

The days that followed were hot and dry, the same as almost every July in Knoxville. The tomato plants in Beverly Welch's backyard were withered and drooping. Caitlin knew exactly how they felt. For two days in a row it was all she could do to raise her head off the pillow to greet each sun-splashed day. Farmers prayed for rain. She prayed for gloom to match her spirits.

Her mother begged her to call Beau. Caitlin steadfastly refused. She wouldn't even go near her apartment for fear that he might be next door. She just couldn't think of facing him.

He obviously didn't want to see her, either. He hadn't tried to contact her. Her mother had called his Knoxville office, and Molly had sent someone over to pick up the rental car. The next day a messenger had delivered Caitlin's clothes. So she knew he had her mother's address. If he wanted to see her, he knew where she was.

*But why should he want to see her?*

She didn't torture herself with unanswerable questions. In fact, she thought she'd be fine if she could just forget his last, shattered expression. He had looked so...so lost. Clearly, the hurts inflicted by his parents had gone much deeper than she had imagined. She hoped he and his father had worked everything out after she had left. But if not...

She didn't like to think about that possibility. Beau's world had been crashing around him, and she had just left. She, who had always been so protective of those she loved, had simply turned her back and walked away.

But what could she have done to help him?

Nothing, of course. Beau didn't love her, despite his protests to the contrary, and he hadn't needed her any longer. Of course, if she had agreed to Richter's crazy scheme, she would have helped his business. But she hadn't. She had left. And now she was plagued by guilt. Even though she hated the way Beau had used her, she also didn't like the thought of his losing his business. Some people might have thought it was exactly what he deserved. But Caitlin wasn't just some person. She loved Beau. Despite everything, she wanted his success.

On her third morning at her mother's house, she rose before Beverly. Carefully, she did her hair, her makeup and slipped on one of the more modest dresses she and Brenda had picked out on their shopping spree in Hilton head. By eight, she was dressed and seated at the kitchen table, calmly sipping coffee.

Beverly poured her own mug of coffee and stood beside the table, her expression thoughtful. "I certainly didn't expect to see you up and looking so pretty."

"I have somewhere important to go." Briefly, Caitlin outlined her plan.

Her mother stared at her for moment. Then she dropped a kiss on the top of her head. "That man's lucky, you know."

Caitlin merely shrugged. She was the one who needed some luck for her meeting with Dalton Richter.

The track field was hot and dusty and filled with noise. Children and adults of all sizes and shapes, ages and colors were in the bleachers and on the field. Yet in the midst of the seeming chaos, it was easy for Beau to spot Caitlin. She was near the edge of the track that circled the field, crouched beside a group of six red-shirted youngsters.

While he was still a short distance away, she stood up, and he stopped for a moment just to drink in the sight of her. Her hair fell in an untidy braid down the back of her red T-shirt, and the red baseball cap on her head looked to be several sizes too small. Her blue-jean cutoffs were worn to white patches across her bottom. A delectable sight, Beau decided. Taking a deep breath, he moved closer.

Caitlin was giving a pep talk. "Now what are we going to do out there today?" she asked.

"Try hard!" came the spirited group response.

"And who's gonna win?"

"Everybody!"

"That's right. Now let's go get 'em." She turned, her laughter spilling forth as she swatted the behinds of her fierce competitors before following them across the field. She was so involved that she didn't notice Beau until she almost ran into him.

He had dreaded this moment, dreaded seeing her hazel eyes darken with scorn. But he smiled through his fear and rescued her from stumbling. "Hey, Coach, I understand you could use an extra hugger."

Her breath caught, and those remarkably clear eyes of hers merely widened. "Beau."

"In the flesh."

"How did you know I was—"

"Beau!" Beverly Welch's enthusiastic greeting interrupted Caitlin's question. "Good to see you," she said cheerfully as she held out her hand.

"Same to you," Beau said, but he kissed her cheek instead of taking her hand.

Caitlin glowered at them both. "Mother," she began, but from the stadium loudspeaker came the announcement that the competition was about to begin. With a last disgusted glance at them both, she jogged after her charges.

"Come with me." Grasping Beau's hand, Beverly pulled him toward the finish line. "I'm the one in charge of huggers. And we've got our work cut out for us today."

Beau had phoned Beverly earlier in the week, soon after Richter had called with the news of Caitlin's visit. Her mother had said there was no way Caitlin would see him, but she had suggested a place to meet where Caitlin would never run away. The first session of summer camp was ending at the Curtis Foundation School, and to mark the occasion they always held a mini "Special Olympics" that they called Game Day. Caitlin hadn't missed this event in over ten years, and even though she hadn't worked at the camp this year, she was planning to attend.

Beau would have met Caitlin in jail—as an inmate—if that had been his only chance of being near her. But the opportunity to see her at work with the kids she loved was even better.

She was a joy to watch. Often more excited than the competitors, she jumped and hopped, whooped and hollered, losing her cap over and over. Her braid came undone. Her voice grew hoarse from cheering. Her T-shirt became grimy from the dust and the eager hugs of dozens of small hands. Her energy seemed inexhaustible as she raced from the track to the broad jump and to the track again, shouting encouragement to anyone who faltered. She patched up scratched knees, dispensed water and awarded prizes. It was obvious that she was in her element, and this Caitlin was easier to love than ever.

Beau had expected that much. What he hadn't expected was to become so caught up in the day himself. He quickly learned how these kids could worm their way into a person's heart. It was their openness that hooked you, that and their bravery. For it took courage to try and fail and try again. Joey and Myra, Billy and Beth—Beverly made sure he met all of Caitlin's favorites, the ones she had told him about.

They were determined little athletes, and they competed for the right reason—for the sheer joy of the contest. He could identify with that emotion, even if he'd had no experience with their physical and mental struggles. Like Joey, whom Caitlin had once described as her class clown, he had once been a young boy, pushing his legs to go faster, striving to outdistance the person on his heels. Beau had felt that final burst of speed, that explosion of happiness that comes from winning. But even if he had never won a race, he would have reacted to the sheer, unbridled joy on Joey's face. Eagerly, he caught the boy just beyond the finish line, swinging him upward for a triumphant ride on his shoulders.

Inexplicably, Caitlin felt tears threaten when she saw Beau with Joey. She always cried on Game Day, but the tears usually came later, after the last kid had been cheered across the finish line, the last hug had been given, the last trophy awarded. Private tears were inevitable when you spent a day watching miracles. Today, however, she was tempted to sit down in the dust and sob right in the middle of everything. Biting her lip, she did sit down, not in the dust but on a bench.

"Come on now." Before she could get settled, Beau was beside her, pulling her to her feet. As usual, his smile reached all the way to his green eyes. "No time to rest. Joey wants to make it three in a row in the broad jump, and he wants his favorite coach beside him."

"Beau, what are you—"

"No time to talk now," he cut in, giving her a push toward the center of the field, and as quickly as he had appeared he was gone.

Joey was calling for her, so Caitlin couldn't pursue Beau. He was right, there was indeed no time to rest, no time for tears. And there was definitely no time for a private discussion with the man she loved. But what was he doing here?

He was in cahoots with her mother, of course. But when asked, Beverly would only volunteer a mysterious smile. She was too busy to talk, anyway, as was Beau. Whether it was the sun glinting off his red hair or his open smile or the impossibly loud Hawaiian-print shirt he wore, for some reason the kids gravitated toward him. He was surrounded when they broke for lunch, and he had a similar crowd all afternoon.

Caitlin didn't attempt to get close to him, but she always knew when he was near. In the middle of everything she would look up, and he would send his smile her way, and something inside her would melt. What was that smile and that warm look in his eyes trying to tell her?

Under that gaze, she became conscious of her untidy hair and dusty clothes. She certainly didn't look glamorous. But she didn't care about that today. This was her—the real her—dust and all, and she was glad to be back where she belonged, doing the things that she did best. Oh, there were changes. This morning she had taken the time to pop in her contacts and brush on some mascara. But those changes were superficial. Inside, she was once again the person she had always been. If it weren't for the persistent ache in her heart, she might never even have met Beau Collins.

Silently, she admitted that that was a lie. With or without the heartache, she had been irreversibly changed by her time with Beau. He had taught her that ducklings could be swans and dreams could come true—if only for a while.

She lost him at the end of the day. The field was a confused mass of tired kids clutching ribbons and frazzled parents pointing cameras. When the dust finally cleared, there was just Caitlin and a loyal group who had volunteered to do the cleanup. Trying to convince herself that she hadn't really wanted to see him, she set to work collecting trash from the field.

"Don't you ever rest?"

Beau's voice caused her to drop her half-filled garbage bag. "Where did you come from?"

He grinned. "Same place as you, I guess. A sperm met an egg and—"

Stubbornly, she snatched up her bag and went back to work. "You're still impossible."

"Did you think a week would change me?"

"Did you think a week would make me forget what you did?" The words tore from Caitlin before she could think.

"And what about what you did?" Beau retorted.

"Me?" Her voice rose in an angry squeak. "What did I do?"

"You almost ruined the Plantation House account."

Nonplussed, she fell back a step and dropped her bag again. "But I went to Richter and agreed to do that stupid appearance."

"Yeah, you talked to him *after* I had convinced him to forget that nonsense."

"After?" This time Caitlin gave into the urge to collapse in the dust. "That old coot," she muttered, kicking viciously at a clump of grass. "That two-faced, lecherous old—"

"My sentiments exactly," Beau said, dropping down beside her. "I went barreling into his office myself, ready to do battle over this whole situation. The guy just laughed. He acted as if he never cared about that Florida grand opening. I think he realized it was a dumb idea, and then he was just testing me."

"Testing?"

"Richter hates people he can push around. I bet he was bluffing me, trying to see if I would stand up to him." Beau's smile was rueful. "And I did, all right, in a big way. I believe his secretary thought the roof was coming off. Now I've got the man's account whether I want it or not."

"So I didn't even need to go talk to him?" Caitlin exclaimed, still irritated.

Beau took her hand. She attempted to pull away, but he held on, while she tried not to think how right it felt for him to touch her. How easy it would be to forget how he had used her, especially with his voice sounding so husky and persuasive. "I really appreciate what you tried to do, Caitlin," he told her. "When Richter first called me to say you had been in to see him, I couldn't believe it. You were so angry that night when you left my parents' house."

"What makes you think I'm not still angry?"

He was silent for a moment. "If you're so angry, why did you go to see Richter?"

Steadfastly, she turned away from his bright, knowing gaze. Stubbornly, she refused to answer him.

Beau continued, "After talking to you, the man was all set to go ahead with that dumb appearance. I had to talk him out of it all over again. He's quite taken with you, you know."

Forgetting to remain aloof, Caitlin came up with a few choice phrases to describe how she felt about Richter.

Laughing at her bluntness, Beau said, "Well, it's all over now. You are officially an ex-model, and I can stay in business. Thanks to my father."

She blinked, clearly confused. "Your father? But I thought you just said that Richter—"

"It was my father who advised me to confront Richter. 'Attack,' he said. 'Fight for the man's business—' "

"And since when do you take your father's advice?" Caitlin interrupted.

"Since the night you and I decided to have a screaming match outside the family-room windows."

Beneath the dirt that streaked her cheeks, she colored. Adorably so, Beau thought.

"It was the best thing that ever happened on that veranda," he insisted. "My parents and I had a long talk. I'm not looking for miracles, but maybe things are going to be better with them."

"I'm glad," Caitlin said softly. "They didn't seem like such monsters to me."

"No," he admitted. "They're not anymore, but I kept seeing them the way they used to be." He laughed and shook his head. "You know, I was becoming all the things that I despised about my parents. I wanted to be a big success so that I could prove something to them. And you can't live your life by other people's rules."

She looked at him in surprise. "I thought you knew that, Beau. I thought you were the family rebel."

He shook his head. "That's the most ironic part of the whole business. In my quest to be different from my father, I was becoming just like him—a man wrapped up in his work." Beau took a deep breath and plunged forward. "Then you came along and distracted me. Now I just want to be wrapped up in you."

She started to rise, her mouth thinning into a stubborn line, but Beau caught her arm, holding her still. "You've got to listen to me, Caitlin. I wasn't using you. No matter how well I wanted the photo shoot to go, or how much I needed Richter's account, I'd never use you. I love you."

She twisted away from him. "Don't say that."

"But it's true. I love you."

She pushed herself to her knees, and her eyes were very wide and very dark. "How can you love me? We barely know each other."

Beau got to his knees also, so that they were both kneeling in the dust. "That's what I thought, that's why I didn't tell you how I felt before. I knew you wouldn't believe the feelings that I had." His voice grew deeper. "But how long does it really take to fall in love, Caitlin? Is there a rule? All I know is that what I feel for you is real."

"But why—"

With a quick movement, Beau brought her into his arms, and though he expected her to protest, she didn't. "Don't ask me why I love you," he murmured, his lips near hers. "I've had nothing but trouble since I fell through your window."

*"You've* had trouble?" she protested, trying to pull away. .

He held her steady. "The worst kind."

"But—"

He silenced her last feeble protest with a kiss. And as usual, streams of color and sensation rocketed through Caitlin. She drew away, touching his face with hands that trembled. Somehow she had to believe what he was saying was true. She had to believe he was really the decent and honest man she had fallen in love with. "Oh, Beau—"

"The worst trouble and the most fun of my life," he whispered, and kissed her again. "Tell me you've had fun, too, Caitlin. It could be like that forever."

Trying to muster the last of her defenses, she said, "I'm not the person who posed in those ads, you know—"

"Please." Beau slid his hands to her shoulders and gave her a little shake. "Give me some credit for brains. I don't care about that woman. This is the Caitlin I want." His fingers caught in her tangled hair. "It's what's inside of you that I love." His eyes, which could be so teasing, were very somber, almost pleading. "Please, Caitlin, say you'll give me a chance."

Every last bit of hesitation drained from Caitlin. "Oh, Beau, I love you so much."

He came to his feet with a whoop then, dragging her with him, pulling her off her feet and spinning her around and around. The dust rolled under his feet, and Caitlin could taste it in his kiss. But that didn't matter. Nothing mattered but being in his arms.

He finally set her down. "Marry me," he muttered huskily. "Soon." He kissed her again, hard. "Tomorrow."

"On one condition," she said, laughing.

"Anything."

"You have to keep getting me modeling jobs."

His eyes grew wide. "You're kidding? I thought you didn't like being just another pretty face."

"Every once in a while it does a woman good to be appreciated on a purely superficial level."

"Give me half a chance, lady," Beau said, laughing. "And I'll appreciate you on every level you can imagine."

"Sounds intriguing." She tipped her head back so that her mouth was inches from his. "But I need to know just one more thing—why did it take you a whole week to find me and explain all of this?"

"I needed romantic surroundings."

"Romantic?" Caitlin glanced around at the bare, dusty track field. Then she looked down at their own sloppy, dirty clothes. "This is romantic?"

His grin was pure Beau—slow, smug, irresistible. "Considering that we started our relationship with me in the bathtub, what's so bad about my proposing in the dirt?"

Before she could reply, the sun dipped low in the sky. And for the briefest of moments, the field was bathed in the purest of shimmering summer sunlight. In that light, even dust turned to gold. But Caitlin didn't think it matched the brilliance of Beau's loving gaze.

"You're right," she murmured. "This isn't bad at all," she murmured and lifted her lips for his kiss.

* * * * *

Silhouette Special Edition

# COMING NEXT MONTH

**#535 NO SURRENDER—Lindsay McKenna**
Navy pilot Alyssa Trayhern's assignment with arrogant jet jockey Clay Cantrell threatens her pride, her career—and her heart—with a crash landing. Book Two of Lindsay McKenna's gripping LOVE AND GLORY series.

**#536 A TENDER SILENCE—Karen Keast**
Former POW Kell Chaisson knew all about survival. He'd brave Bangkok's dangers to help Anne Elise Butler trace her MIA husband's fate, but would he survive loving another man's wife?

**#537 THORNE'S WIFE—Joan Hohl**
Jonas Thorne was accomplished, powerful, devastatingly attractive. Valerie Thorne loved her husband, but what would it take to convince domineering Jonas that she was a person, not simply his wife?

**#538 LIGHT FOR ANOTHER NIGHT—Anne Lacey**
Wildlife biologist Brittany Hagen loved the wolves on primeval Isle Svenson . . . until she encountered the two-legged variety—in the person of ferociously attractive, predatory Paul Johnson.

**#539 EMILY'S HOUSE—Nikki Benjamin**
Vowing to secretly support widowed Emily Anderson and her child, Major Joseph Cortez rented rooms in her house. But, hiding a guilty secret, could he ever gain entrance to Emily's heart?

**#540 LOVE THIS STRANGER—Linda Shaw**
Pregnant nutritionist Mary Smith unwittingly assumed another woman's identity when she accepted a job with the Olympic ski team. Worse, she also "inherited" devastating Dr. Jed Kilpatrick—the other woman's lover!

---

# AVAILABLE THIS MONTH:

**#529 A QUESTION OF HONOR**
Lindsay McKenna

**#530 ALL MY TOMORROWS**
Debbie Macomber

**#531 KING OF HEARTS**
Tracy Sinclair

**#532 FACE VALUE**
Celeste Hamilton

**#533 HEATHER ON THE HILL**
Barbara Faith

**#534 REPEAT PERFORMANCE**
Lynda Trent